Advance Praise for
Gunshots in Grudgeville

"Landis is a master of her craft. These stories sing—with struggle and surrender, with humanity and hope. They'll change the way you see the people of the rural Midwest."

—Kim Suhr, author of *Nothing to Lose* (Cornerstone Press, 2018)

"Laurel Landis takes us into a world of small-town characters that make us laugh and break our hearts. These are people we knew and loved and are happy to meet again in her stories."

—Carol Wobig, author of *The Collected Stories* (Hidden Timber Books, 2017)

"*Gunshots in Grudgeville* is a wonderful collection—full, varied, and a showcase for Laurel Landis's considerable talents: her eye for precise, evocative details, often those centering on small-town life; her insight into human relationships and their emotional complexities; and per-haps greatest of all, her ability to reveal how profound and universal the small, quiet moments of our individual lives can be."

—Larry Watson, author of *Montana 1948*, *American Boy*, As *Good As Gone*, and *Let Him Go*

GUNSHOTS IN GRUDGEVILLE

and Other Stories

LAUREL J. LANDIS

Ten|16
PRESS

www.ten16press.com - Waukesha, WI

For Joe,
I'll always be with you.

CONTENTS

INTRODUCTION

I grew up in a village with just six streets. Some, like the street I lived on, were only a block long. Others were bits of country roads that bore names only where they passed through town. A tiny, self-contained world, with all the landmarks of a small midwestern community—a school, constantly threatened with closing, a town hall hosting everything from funeral lunches to wedding suppers and meetings of the local Legionnaires. The grocery store that sat in the center of town remains to this day. It has always been there, and has always doubled as something else—a shoe store, a laundromat, and finally, a café. And the village was circled by lush woods and broad fields, green in spring and gold in the fall.

I was surrounded by family. My grandmother lived next door, and aunts, uncles, and cousins' houses dotted the rest of the village. Family enough to see what kind of trouble I might be getting into and report it to my mother, but also to make sure I was safe or give me a treat to take home.

In many ways, my childhood was idyllic. I was safe and sheltered. Untethered by technology that didn't exist yet, I spent my days exploring the woods, where pine cones and leaf boats replaced my need for screen time, or store-bought toys. Between lunch and dinner I roamed, and again after supper. I explored every house, backyard, and woodland until the streetlights lit up the ends of my block.

As a teen, I began to feel a keen sense of the limitations of small-town life. I wanted—needed—to see what I could find beyond those six streets. As soon as I could, I left, sure I would never return. But a love of place, family, and the pastoral beauty I grew up with had planted a seed in me, one that only bloomed after a decade in New York City and half a lifetime. I found myself back home in spirit and in my writing life.

I like to think I linger there, in that magical place, swimming in the lake in the dark, carefree, dreaming of my future.

These stories are fiction, and none of the incidents are true. However, many of the people in these stories share characteristics of those I knew. I hope they speak to you, through all their flaws and successes, as they still do to me.

TORNADO

Cousin Gaylord was an alcoholic. Not the kind who lives quietly in the shadows of the local bar, listening to a country jukebox and the crack of dice. No, Gaylord was a *spectacular* alcoholic, whose mistakes were as hard to ignore as his successes.

We swore him off. We wouldn't answer the phone at 2:00 a.m. or pick him up at the county jail. Mom wouldn't lend him money. But we didn't stick to it. On the one hand, we felt sorry for him. On the other, we couldn't help wanting to see what kind of twisted situation he'd gotten himself into.

There was a time he sobered up, got a job in the city. To our surprise, and even Gaylord's, it turned out that along with his natural charm and amiability, he was a bit of a genius. Despite a lack of higher education, he invented something important, a breakthrough innovation he said, and was moved off the plant floor to his own office. He bought a house with a pool, new cars, and gifts for all the relatives, which he handed out on visits home. Big things, like new TVs, fancy appliances. Dad wouldn't take any of them, except a few kitchen gadgets for Mom.

Gaylord hung onto that job for fifteen years. Then suddenly, mysteriously, he was laid off. Sometime after that, he ended up in a church in his underwear in the middle of the day. The *Pine County Journal* covered it, just as they'd written up his winning touchdowns and his invention at the plant. Those stories filled long columns next to various class photos, and were kept in the family scrapbook.

"Something must have happened to make him start up again," Mom said.

"What makes you think he ever left off? Got good at hiding it is all," said Aunt Jo.

My mother opened the paper again and again, but the picture remained the same: Gaylord, wrapped in a policeman's jacket, being led out of St. Peter's Cathedral, wild-eyed and barefoot.

After that, he began to take odd jobs. None of them lasted long. There were just some things he couldn't put up with, he said. He started showing up at our house on weekends, in some kind of jam, or just drunk and wanting Dad to go out with him. Dad never would, even if he might have if someone else had been asking. The next day, we'd hear Gaylord had gotten in a fight, or hit a deer, or fallen out of a window and broken a leg, which you'd think would have stopped him, but it didn't. He drank with a cane in one hand and a beer in the other, and then he drank with a limp.

He was fifty years old now, and it looked like being a drunk was going to be his final occupation. There was no sign he'd had enough; then again, neither had we. Gaylord was a bad habit. We were hooked.

It was the week before the July Fourth celebration. The town was brimming with tourists and out-of-town relatives. They lined up at Johnson's Market, their arms full of six-packs and hot dogs; jostled for parking spaces with the locals. Spare bedrooms were filled, and RVs and campers were parked in driveways to hold the overflow. In our house, there was only Mom's younger brother, Uncle Mike. Six feet two of him scrunched onto the couch at night, his canvas bag in the corner by the back door. Mike was closer to my age than my mom's and felt more like a big brother than my uncle. I worshipped him.

"Aaand the screen door slams," Mom said, "*again*."

A sharp, sour smell came in, and then there was Gaylord, all boisterous and happy, a drunken kind of happy with hysterical lining up behind it. Normally this wouldn't have stopped the card game we'd begun after supper. But there was a stranger, too. A woman.

"This is Debbie," he said, beaming like she was a brand-new appliance he'd found on the side of the road and couldn't believe his luck.

"She's a real lady," he said. "She's a keeper."

Mike cleared his throat.

She stretched out an arm to Dad and flopped her hand into his.

She was quiet, soft-spoken. And she was clearly Gaylord's age, which made her too-tight jeans, tank top, and high heels all the more puzzling. The manner didn't match the clothes.

There were hugs all around.

"These are my favorite people in the whole world," Gaylord told Debbie.

Dad shifted on his feet and put his hands in his pockets.

Mike snorted.

"Nice to meet you," Debbie said, her voice only a little above a whisper.

"What?" asked Dad.

"He's deaf," Mom told Debbie. "Come on, Mike, put those cards away."

She offered lemonade to the visitors. The vapor of liquor and perfume they'd brought in with them was overpowering in our small house, still stuffy from the heat of the afternoon. None of us wanted them to sit. We needn't have worried. The threat of lemonade kept them upright.

"What are you doing in town, Gaylord?" Dad asked.

"We're celebrating," he said, glancing at Debbie, "on account of I've got some news."

He started to smile, but his face screwed up in the process. A couple tears broke out and started down his cheeks. Debbie studied the dining room.

"I'm coming home for good. I'm living in Mercy Lake now—"

"Well!" Mom interrupted. "That's wonderful news!"

"Up at the shack mostly," he finished, accepting a tissue from my mother and wiping his nose.

Mom's mouth snapped shut. He meant the hunting shack. It didn't have a bathroom, much less a stove or a fridge. I imagined him out there in the woods with a cooler and a campfire. Even for Gaylord, it didn't sound like a move in the right direction.

"Did you quit your job again, Gay?" Dad asked.

I knew that tone of voice. I'd have changed the subject.

Gaylord didn't notice, just kept talking, like living at the hunting shack was no big deal. "I *retired*, Marty!" he said, slapping Dad on the back. "I'm my own boss now."

Dad picked his teeth with a toothpick. "How you going to make a living? How you going to eat?"

"I've got my hands in a couple businesses," Gaylord said in a singsongy way. "Heck, Marty, stop worrying. I ain't broke. Come on down to the bar with us. I'll buy you a beer. Hell, I'll buy as much as you can hold." He waited for Debbie to chime in, but she was fixated on a little Indian doll with black braids and a real leather tunic that sat on the top shelf of the curio cabinet. I wanted to tell her that no matter how wistfully she looked at it, Mom was not going to offer her that doll. It had been there, next to a miniature teacup and saucer, since before I was born.

Dad said no like he always did, and I felt kind of bad for both of them, like I always did. As soon as they'd gone, Mike turned the fan up to high speed.

Mom was optimistic. "Maybe it will do him some good, being back home," she said.

Everyone went quiet, as though considering whether it would do Gaylord good. No one could muster any support for it. Dad returned to his chair in the living room and unmuted the television.

"Well," Mom said, mostly to herself, "he can't get into much trouble here."

But then Gaylord met Cliff Black.

Cliff was a drunk, too, of a very different sort. Unpredictable, dangerous, given to bouts of violence when things didn't go his way. That's what people said. Dad said Cliff was not the kind of man whose eye you wanted to catch. If you wanted to look at him, and everybody did, you'd better be doing it from behind his back.

I saw Cliff and Gaylord sometimes, sitting together in the window of Klugman's Bar, or at the beach, sticking out on the sand among the little kids and the college girls. I recognized the pair, one dark-haired, one light, both of them fully dressed and sunglassed with a cooler between them I knew held no lemonade.

I supposed that for a drunk to meet another drunk must be a wonderful thing, kind of a relief, and I was glad Gaylord had a friend. I was optimistic.

The night before the holiday celebration, I snuck out to the back step to listen to the firecrackers, echoing from all the corners of town. Above me, Mom and Dad's bedroom windows were dark. I smoked a cigarette, and listened, and watched the occasional car sweep down Main Street.

Main Street began at the school, dark and quiet now, and dipped past our house to the end of the block where a streetlight lit up the curve. It curved to the left until it wound around the lake and out of town.

Jason Anderson lived on that road in the summers, in a big house on the hill overlooking the water. Jason was something rare in Mercy Lake, with his green eyes and curly hair, and a general air of carefree I lusted after but didn't understand. He hung out with the town girls whose parents worked and who could stay at the beach after sundown. My friends were my schoolmates, most of them from the farms outside of town. In the summer, they stayed home, working in the fields and in the barns, riding horses. They had big families. They didn't need town.

Sometimes, Jason talked to me when I ran into him at the post office or the grocery. Once, he asked when I was going to grow up so he could take me out. I decided I'd wait for that, forsaking any other offers. And wait I had, though it hadn't been hard because even though I'd turned sixteen in January and was old enough to date, I hadn't been asked. The only boys I knew I'd known my whole life. The only *people* I knew I'd known my whole life, except in the summer when Mercy Lake's population swelled from a hopeful 273 to well over a thousand. Visitors stayed at the campgrounds and appeared in town piecemeal until the holiday week when they all came at once. Kayakers, motor boaters, water-skiers—a strange breed to us who'd grown up there and didn't see the point of all that fancy gear. They were good-looking people with shorts and t-shirts that, from a needle-and-thread standpoint, were the same as ours. But there's a difference between clothes worn with an ironic sense of fun and recreation and those worn to save your good clothes for the school year.

City people came to Mercy Lake because there's nothing like a small-town Independence Day, Dad said, and there aren't many small towns left.

On July third, the neighbor's daughter cleaned out her closet.

"Thought this might fit you, Gilly," she said.

She handed me a grocery bag. I lifted out a pale blue dress with spaghetti straps and butterflies embroidered on the skirt. It fit perfectly.

The dress was a good omen. This year, I would be carefree, too. No one would know I was a local or that I hadn't had a date yet.

The holiday began with people in and out of the house every five minutes. Relatives, Legionnaires, townies.

"If one more person slams that door," Mom said. Pots of barbecue overwhelmed the top of her tiny stove. She wouldn't let us touch it.

"Gilly! Leave it," she said and gave me a playful push. "You'll have to buy a sandwich from the Ladies Auxiliary booth."

It made no sense to have to buy food from my own mother, but arguing was futile. Mike got out the cereal bowls, complaining about guests having to do their own cooking.

At precisely 11:30, we gathered our folding chairs and took our places along the street. Mike slipped me a beer in a koozie.

"It's a holiday," he said.

It was hot, hotter than July had been in years. By noon, the temperature was ninety-five. Mike and I rigged umbrellas over the heads of the older aunts to protect them from heatstroke. They talked and poked at one another, until the sound of snare drums echoed from behind the school. We leaned forward in our lawn chairs.

I caught a glimpse of Cliff and Gaylord, standing across the street, and strained to see between the long-haired girls of the Hands Up Church.

"What a mighty God we serve," they sang. "Angels bow before him. Heaven and earth adore him. What a mighty God we serve!"

They smiled a lot to show us how happy they were. I smiled back.

"They've got candy!" screamed a little boy. I leapt out after him as the girls threw handfuls onto the street.

"I can't eat the taffy!" Jo yelled.

I grabbed a fistful of whatever I could, to help the little ones out.

"Gilly! Get the root beer barrel!" yelled Jo.

"Geez," I said, catching it as it rolled toward the gutter.

I handed her the barrel, putting the rest in the paper sack a little boy held out.

Cliff and Gaylord flickered in the heat as the American flag dragged its shadow over the sidewalk.

I didn't understand how a person could be loyal to a whole country. But the war, Dad's war, was sacred. I knew because he never talked about it. There were only three of the guys left this year. He marched past in his uniform, rifle swinging precisely from shoulder to chest, calling out orders. He looked like he knew what he was doing, like he'd known what he was doing all along, and that was why we'd won.

"Now why doesn't Gaylord have his hand over his heart? After his dad was in the service and all," said Aunt Jo.

"Cliff does. Look," I said.

"Yeah, with a beer in it."

"Still," I said.

Cliff saw me looking and raised his glass. My cheeks got hot.

The sheriff's car appeared, signaling the end of the parade. We folded up our chairs and left them leaning against a tree.

Ten minutes later, the parade hit the lakefront, spilling out of formation and into the open space in front of the pavilion, which had been transformed into a flag the size of a building. Red and white streamers flowed from its roof, and a bandstand at one end was hung with shiny silver stars on a blue background. A long bar stretched the length of it, already flanked by people standing three deep. There was a lot of smell to take in: roasted hot dogs, corn on the cob, sweet hay sprinkled around the grounds. Tufts of cotton candy had been dropped and were covered with ants and dirt, turning to syrup in the heat.

I scanned the crowd for Jason as we made our way through the clumps of strangers, the piglet raceway, the stacked poles in front of the Big Blue Fish pond.

"We'd better buy a barbecue," Mike said. We found Mom at the Ladies Auxiliary booth, and I handed back the five-dollar bill she'd given me that morning.

"I'm going to look around," said Mike. He was looking for a girl just as I was looking for a boy.

A group of kids scoured an impossible mound of sand for pennies. Mike swung Paul Bunyan's hammer.

No Jason.

I dropped a pole in the fish pond and gave a toy trout to a kid too short to fish.

No Jason.

The afternoon passed, hot and lazy, and a dark cloud flowered in my chest. I told myself it wasn't over yet. There was still a chance. It was the best chance in all of summer, a guarantee. The fireworks.

At five o'clock, we helped Mom put her pots in cardboard boxes and lugged them home to rest a while before gathering up our sparklers and aunts for the return to the lake.

"Take a jacket," said Mom, and laughed at herself.

"If it were any hotter, Evelyn, you'd have to peel us out of here," Mike said.

The whole town was headed in the same direction, house lights darkening one by one as the crowd thickened on the way. Cars and people spilled onto the roads around the lake and all the way up the hill behind it where the Andersons lived in summers, in a big house with a pool and a trampoline. They seemed like millionaires, because the rest of us lived in vinyl-sided boxes in a constant state of disrepair. The minute a family started trying to fix one up, the mill would have a layoff. It could be years that a house would have all new windows on one side and half the roof shingled, and tar paper on the other getting soaked in the rain and tearing in the winter wind, until the owners saved enough to make it right, and then it would look out of place.

We arranged the blankets and a couple of the smaller cousins in a cluster in front of us and settled in as the first boom sounded.

The best part of fireworks is the *whoompf* they make when they get shot out of the tubes. That's what I said.

Mike said no, it's the crackly sound they make when they rain down into the treetops.

And suddenly I knew where Jason was. Out on the water, in the Andersons' boat. An unmistakable boat, too big for our little lake. Between explosions, when the wind was just right, I could hear the clinking of ice cubes and the soft, elegant tone of their voices reaching all the way to shore. *Of course he wouldn't miss the fireworks*, I thought. He just had a better way of seeing them.

"It looks like my peonies exploded," said Aunt Jo.

We timed the finale at exactly ninety seconds. When the last ember drifted into the bushes with a little parachute of yellow smoke, the older folks took the little ones and started for home.

"You want to stay here a while with your Uncle Mikey?" joked Mike, nudging me.

I was sixteen now, and though unsure of what the new rules might be, I understood it should include a later curfew. I also understood that Mike wanted to flirt with the Lewises' oldest girl without it seeming to be his whole purpose, making me a prop. I didn't mind. After all, so was he.

"Check it out," he said and handed me a big plastic cup, undisguised this time, with beer foam spilling out over the top.

"Pretty obvious," I said.

"Nobody's going to care. Blame it on me."

It tasted like the Fourth of July.

And then I saw Jason, taller than last summer, in khaki shorts and leather sandals, his face illuminated in the little pool of light coming from the popcorn wagon.

"I'll be right back," I said.

"Go get him," said Mike, raising his glass in a salute of encouragement. I took a few gulps of beer and pushed my way through the people.

"Hey!" I said.

Jason turned around.

"Hey, Gilly." He smiled. "How are you?"

"Okay," I said and got out some change to buy popcorn even though I didn't want any. He asked for two bags. I put the change back in my purse.

"What are you drinking?" he asked, leaning over to peer into my glass.

"Having a beer," I said.

"You're too young, I think," he said.

I shrugged. "Lots of people are."

Mrs. Moss, who was working the wagon, handed Jason two bags. And then a tall blonde girl with long legs and a suntan walked up next to Jason and grabbed his hand. She looked down at me blankly.

He gave the girl a bag of popcorn and then walked away without even looking back. "Hey, don't drink too much of that, now."

I tugged at my dress, which somehow seemed to blame, and tried to hold my face steady, like nothing had happened.

I told Mike about it.

"Ah, he's a piece of crap anyway. I heard he can't read. Slow or something."

"He is?" I was doubtful.

Mike nodded. I gulped down the bitter beer. At least I had that.

"Hey, it's a holiday," he said, slapping me on the back. "Give me a handful of that, and I'll take you out for a polka."

I handed him the popcorn I'd had to buy for myself.

Even hours after sundown, the heat hadn't let up. The concrete dance floor under the pavilion was chaos. Couples bumped around the perimeter, vying for the spot in front of the bandstand. In the afternoon, there'd been heavy metal. Now, with the college kids gone out to the bars on Highway T, we were left with Wild Oats, whose lead singer was so fat his lower half hung over the side of what I could only guess was a stool, his legs camped out in front of his body like two huge sleeping bears, his feet forming tiny snouts. Even his sneakers strained at the laces. But he could sing like Hank Williams, Mike said, and that trumps fat.

"Christ, I've got to sit," said Mike. "Let's get us a beer, shall we?"

He got two beers, and we went back to our table.

"Look," he said, leaning into me. "Black."

"Where?" I asked. He nodded at one of the picnic tables set up a few feet off to the side of the bar.

I watched as Cliff got out his trademark bottle of whiskey and set it on the table. Looks were exchanged around the bar, but no one moved in his direction. No one wanted to make him mad.

Cliff had been one of the best-looking people ever raised in Mercy Lake, judging from the pictures I'd seen. He could have been a movie star, with his black hair and his deep, dark eyes set in a chiseled face. Then right out of high school, he fell into a whiskey bottle and never came out, and I guess the point was it damaged his looks. The rumor said he'd run over someone back then with his old Plymouth, left them to die on the road, and spent a year in prison. After that, he stuck to beating his girlfriends like everybody else. From a distance, Cliff was still lean and young. It was an illusion.

Dad said Cliff was a ruined wreck of a man. I couldn't stop looking at him, though I'd been warned.

"Whoa," said Mike. "Look at Gaylord's little angel. She can put it away."

Debbie had changed. She wasn't quiet and polite anymore. She was laughing too loud, downing whiskey straight from the bottle. I strained to see Gaylord, but only Cliff was at the table, watching the women around him get wilder as they drank, egging them on when he could.

"The guy's like a farmer at a cock fight," said Mike.

Cliff took the bottle and set it down, and Debbie reached for it. He laughed, lifted and moved it a little farther away. She threw her whole torso onto the table to retrieve it, cursing at him loud enough to be heard over the steel guitar. Once she had a good hold on the bottle, she took it with her to the dance floor, holding it delicately out to the side, her other hand resting on her stomach, fingers splayed out across her ribs, wide hips gyrating a beat slower than the music. The air was thick and hot, and the whole place was pungent with beer and sweat and cigarettes. Her eyes were closed. Every few beats or so, she fell slightly off-balance. The other couples gave her plenty of room, pretending not to notice, but a drunken woman with a whiskey bottle is almost as good as a dirty movie and just as hard not to watch, Mike said. When the song ended with a few heavy, slowing drumbeats and a downward twang of the guitar, she sprang into momentary consciousness, raising her free hand in slow motion.

"Whoo-hoo!" she cried. The effort caused her to stagger backward a step. She drew the bottle to her lips and emptied it, and then set it with great care on the edge of the table. The band struck up a ballad, and back she went, swaying toward a tall man built like a mattress with big, slow eyes. He swayed forward. Even a dimwit knows an opportunity like that, and the minute they were within a foot of each other, his hands began to roam, first along her back, then lower and lower by inches. She grabbed his face with her hands and let his big bear lips cover hers.

"Wow!" I said, and Mike laughed so hard he sputtered a little beer out his nose.

"Romeo and Juliet," he said. "Wait 'til Gaylord sees that."

Cliff saw it, and so did his girlfriend, who put a hand on his arm. She looked anxiously toward the bar, where Gaylord stood, his back to the dance floor. Cliff shrugged and brushed her off.

We held our breath, sitting still, ears back like dogs watching squirrels.

Gaylord covered the distance in a couple of steps.

Mike lowered his beer. "Uh-oh."

Gaylord grabbed Debbie's elbow. She pulled it away. Another grab, another pull. He wheeled around to Cliff.

"Should have been watching her," was all I heard.

Cliff looked bored. And the whiskey bottle, no longer anchored by its contents, was bumped and bounced out of place onto the concrete floor. Cliff reached into a bag and got out another bottle. The men at the bar straightened a little, but when Debbie stalked off toward the porta-potties with Gaylord in hot pursuit, they relaxed and returned to their drinks.

"Aw, man," I said.

"Don't worry. That's not going to be the end of it. Bar's open 'til two," said Mike. "Listen, I'll be right back. Here." He handed me a few dollars. "Get yourself something." He went to try again with Mary Lewis.

My friends had left with their families after the fireworks. I imagined them at home now in the country with the moonlight on the pasture, the smell of sweet clover wafting in through their bedroom windows. You couldn't be lonely there, with the wind and the crickets. Jason Anderson wouldn't matter. Wouldn't even make a ripple in the tall grass.

I made my way to the bar, careful to avoid eye contact with adults. I didn't want to be asked about my folks or how I liked having my driver's license. The vision of farm life began to recede, along with the promise of excitement. The lights of the pavilion blurred.

"Gillygirl, Gillygirl, where is your daddy?"

Cliff Black, leaning on the bar with his elbows, folded his hands and looked straight at me.

"Over at the Legion booth, I guess," I said.

"I'm surprised he let you out," he said.

I sort of giggled. I shouldn't have, I knew that, but I couldn't help it.

"What are you drinking?" he asked, as if he didn't know.

I shrugged.

"Hang on a second," he said.

He took my cup with him to the table where he'd been sitting. I'd only had whiskey once before, stolen out of my parents' liquor cabinet when they'd been out. It was exciting then, too.

I took a cigarette out of my purse and looked around.

"Aw, nobody's lookin'," said Cliff.

"Dad'll kill me if he sees," I said, and Cliff got a lighter out of his pocket and lit my cigarette like a gentleman.

"Well, Gillygirl," he said, "sometimes you gotta do things your daddy don't like."

Mike was at the other end of the bar, leaning over it, smiling at Mary who'd given up her hot dog post and come to have a beer with him. Only a girl could cause Mike to be hatless.

"Where's your boyfriend?" Cliff asked.

I shook my head. "No boys around here." I felt like I was going to cry.

"Now that's a shame, that is. Girl your age should have a boyfriend. Take you out to the movies."

I slugged down the whiskey. He laughed.

"Gimme," he said, and I surrendered my cup. He got me some more whiskey, this time with no Coke in it.

He said he used to like to dance, but the army gave him a bum leg, and he couldn't do it anymore. Otherwise, he would have taken me out for a spin.

"Mom said you hurt your leg in a car accident," I ventured.

"You always believe what your parents tell you?"

"No," I said.

"Thing is, Gilly, town like this, people talk a lot of shit. Nothin' else to do."

He's right, I thought. Thinking it made me feel guilty.

"Nothing against your parents. It ain't their fault. They're just goin' by what they hear. Now you, you're a smart kid. I got a feeling you already know that."

And he was right about people in Mercy Lake and about me being smart, but he didn't think I was a kid, I could tell that. He looked down at my dress.

It wasn't sex that scared me. It was something else, something dark I couldn't put a name to. Something Cliff had in spades.

"People think you're a bad influence," I said.

For a second, he looked confused. And then he took his cigarette out of his mouth and laughed out loud, his eyes twinkling black like a starless sky.

"What on? Gaylord? How much influence do you think I have on anybody?" And the thing was I understood that, too. Now that he'd said it, I knew it was true. Close up, he was an old man, his hair streaked with gray, skin pale, eyes bloodshot, sad. In fact, it occurred to me that the only difference between the two men was that Cliff wasn't part of our family.

"Let me put it this way. I live my life. I don't bother nobody. Then Gaylord comes along, doin' what he's always done, and people think I'm a bad influence. People think I chase him down and empty that bottle down his throat. Is that what you think?"

"What do you care what I think?"

"I'll tell you what. I don't know that I do."

I'd never been talked to quite like that before. It made me queasy, like I was walking on the ice too late in spring, waiting to hear the crack.

"Don't take it personally," he said. He looked friendly when he laughed.

I laughed back, feeling better than I had all day.

"Speak of the devil," said Cliff as Gaylord walked up to the bar.

Gaylord stood still, staring, his face stony and unfamiliar.

"What's your problem?" Cliff asked.

"What the hell is the matter with you?" Gaylord looked at my cup. "She ain't old enough to drink that shit."

"She can handle it. This here is a smart young lady," said Cliff and winked at me. I smiled.

Gaylord ignored me.

Cliff turned back to the bar and took a sip of his drink, bent down close to my ear. "Time for you to go, Gill," he said.

I moved away from the bar.

"I said she ain't old enough."

Cliff turned to face Gaylord.

"Bet she's old enough for a lot of things she ain't done yet," he said.

"You're crossing a line, Black."

"What line is that?"

"You know what line."

"Shit, Gaylord, I ain't crossed a line in twenty years," Cliff said, laughing, and I believed him.

Out of the blue, Gaylord swung like a blind man, recklessly missing my head by half an inch. I ducked. Cliff ducked. Gaylord started pushing him, and Cliff pushed back limply, like he didn't have it in him.

At first, the band just kept going. We didn't take it seriously because, even though Gaylord's face was getting redder by the second, Cliff was still laughing. I figured the cops would be there any minute, up from the beach where the tourists were trying to blow their hands off with firecrackers. Seemed everyone figured that and was waiting to see if interference was really going to be necessary.

"That's it, Gaylord. Hoooo-ey! Show 'em what you're made of."

At this Gaylord threw a punch. The crowd backed off. Cliff put his hands up to block it, but he was too drunk to put up much of a fuss. He couldn't get his balance back and staggered backward, ending up half sitting on the edge of a picnic table. A push, a slap. Cliff didn't seem to care. My own fists curled in on themselves on his behalf. Finally, he tired of it and threw his own punch. It was a mistake.

Gaylord's nose began to bleed. He smiled, blood ran into his mouth, and suddenly the world fast-forwarded itself. He picked up the whiskey bottle and brought it down on the side of Cliff's face like he was chopping wood, and the man in black rolled off the table onto the floor, his head hitting the cement with a loud crack.

Then everything slowed way down. The band sputtered to a stop. The crowd gathered around Gaylord, still cursing and swinging his arms. When those had been harnessed by two old Legionnaires, he kicked until, finally, a third man simply dragged Cliff out of his reach.

Gaylord grinned.

I could have sworn I didn't know him, nor he me. He was someone whose eye I didn't want to catch.

A cop ran toward us, pulling a radio off his belt as he jogged. I felt a tug at my arm.

Cliff wasn't moving.

"Gilly!" said Mike. "Come on." He tossed his beer with a plonk onto the ground and grabbed my wrist, pulling me along through the crowd, all townies now. I wondered when the city people had left and where they'd gone.

"Evelyn?" Mike went halfway up the stairs, so he didn't have to shout. "Evelyn, can you come down here a minute?"

Mom stepped carefully down the carpeted stairs, tying her robe.

"What? What is it? It's late."

She eyed me, but if she thought I'd been drinking, she didn't say anything.

Mike began to tell the story and stopped in the middle as Dad came into the kitchen, closing the screen door gently.

"Marty? What in the world?" Mom asked.

Dad's eyes were bloodshot, but he was sober as a judge. He shook his head, bewildered.

"Sheriff's right behind me." He held his Legion cap in both hands.

The screen door banged.

Sheriff Hofstedt nodded to Dad.

"Marty. It ain't good," he said, holding a pause as if to wait until we were ready to hear what he had to say.

"Cliff Black's gone. Pronounced him at the scene. Got about a hundred witnesses saw Gaylord hit him. There's just nothing to be done now but wait. Outcome's going to be bad."

I wished I didn't have all the whiskey in my head because it felt like the air was too still and the sky too yellow, even though we were indoors.

Mom said it was a good thing, that Cliff was already kind of a vegetable, that he had it coming. The blood rushed to my face.

"I knew that man was trouble." She wiped her eyes with the sleeve of her robe. "Poor Gay!"

I opened my mouth, but nothing came out. Mike shot me a warning glance.

"Wasn't Cliff's fault, Evelyn," the sheriff said.

Mom blinked.

"Gaylord was a goddamned tornado," he said. "Sooner or later, it's gonna do some damage."

Early Sunday morning, I snuck a beer from the cooler in the garage to help put a headache to rest—and another to help me think—concealed them in my backpack, and walked down to the lake park.

The Andersons' boat was docked, rocking gently in the morning waves. The last of the holiday's firecrackers popped off from time to time somewhere on the other side of the lake. I imagined them, hissing and smoking at the water's edge. Everything was the same as it was before, only it wasn't.

I stayed out of sight on a bench inside the empty pavilion. Most of the garbage had been picked up and bagged, but Cliff's blood was still there, a dark, browning stain on the concrete under plastic cups and cigarette butts. What was left of the whiskey bottle sat in a corner. The police hadn't even bothered to take it, as if it was just another empty bottle and the worst it had done was get somebody drunk.

It dawned on me then that it was a luxury to be a kid, and not upset, with nothing bad to think about on a summer Sunday. And I was not a kid anymore.

OLAGAM

The wind had a peculiar timbre in the pine wood, not like the sound rain made as it passed through deciduous trees, but deeper, like an oboe and, to Jim, ominous. Had the wind carried Gwen's scent to the clearing?

He had to bend a little to see what she'd seen. In the distance, beneath the lower branches of the pine trees, the meadow formed a lush rectangle as green and luminous as moss. He closed his eyes and saw the bear there, imagined the camera click and Gwen, standing still in the forest, focusing the lens as the bear rose up on its hind legs to eat the berries growing at the meadow's edge.

The bear might have moved slowly toward the trees, and Gwen would have tensed, surprised when he entered the woods, close enough for her to see the muscles on his back. She would have stayed quiet and slipped behind a tree, a hand on its craggy bark as she peered around it, still feeling safe. Feeling lucky to see a bear up close.

He zipped his jacket against the wind and walked on to the spot the sheriff had shown him on that first day. Tiny burrs clung to his socks. After a week of heavy gales, branches were strewn over the forest floor, and he had an image, knew what had happened.

A limb had fallen from high up in a tree, landing next to her with a thud and a rustle, and the bear looked up from the fruit. Gwen panicked. She would have known she'd stayed too long, the knowledge flickering across her face as she backed away. But the bear had seen her and ambled casually into the trees. She lost her composure and began to run. It must have happened that way.

The brochure said the town of Olagam was named for a bear in Indian legend. *Now, bears are uncommon this far north on the peninsula,* Jim had read, *where the tourists come in April and stay until the splendor of autumn has passed. Though there is plenty of space for solitude, the villages are always bustling, and a slice of the area's famous cherry pie is always within easy reach.*

And the road, thought Jim, *though it seems remote from here, is only a quarter mile away.*

He forced himself to tread carefully over the weather-whitened pine roots that erupted from the forest floor. He forced himself to walk, not run, past the cabin she'd rented and back to his car, tossing his pack and the rifle onto the passenger seat. Even inside it, he felt no relief, nor any as he parked in the lot behind his hotel, or when he stepped out onto the sidewalk and saw that the shops were still open and busy. Wooden easels held menus, pottery-lined tables on the sidewalks. He inhaled the scent of pressed apples and cinnamon. Two teenage girls bumped him as they pushed out the door of the mercantile. They wore green-and-white aprons over their tank tops, hands already digging in purses for cigarettes.

"Sorry," one of them said. She smiled. The smell of cider seemed to be coming from her mouth. He heard the click of a shutter.

Inside the mercantile, he found the emptiest aisle and stood looking at the display of carved gourds and nature books. *Artists of the Peninsula. The Life of John Muir. Wood Carving.* He chose two of the least challenging books made mostly of pictures, to read later in the hotel while he waited for the next day to come. Jim felt the shopkeeper's eyes on him and dreaded her closeness as she shuffled closer. A damp shock of blonde hair fell over her forehead, and he felt sweat on his own. It was hot inside, away from the lake breeze, the last of the summer still captive inside the store.

"I'm sorry to hear about your wife," the shopkeeper began.

"Thanks," he said, praying she'd stop and feeling his face flush with the effort. He wondered if everyone in the small community knew who he was and why he was there. That meant they'd known Gwen. The shopkeeper hovered.

"She came into the store a lot. And the thing is, she liked those best," she said, pointing at a free-standing rack to his left.

Bears. Tiny shelves filled with bears and, on the top tier, Olagam himself.

"Do you know the story?" she asked.

Jim shook his head.

"Well, in the legend," she said, clearing her throat, "in the legend, Olagam was a good bear. He helped people."

Jim looked up.

"He guided them through the forests." She moved the little wooden statue so it was centered on the shelf. "We haven't had an incident like your wife in twenty years. We just can't figure out what happened. And we're so sorry for your loss."

"I'll take it," he said.

She rolled Olagam in brown paper and put him in a small green bag with straw handles.

"No charge." She handed him the bag.

When he returned to his room, he tossed his rifle on the bed and reached for a can of oil on the nightstand. Instructions for cleaning and polishing were copied on a single sheet of paper, along with crude drawings of the gun's parts. He pulled the plastic cap from the spout and shook some oil onto the rag. There was nothing else to do.

Outside his window, cars turned on their lights as they rounded the curve in front of the harbor, full of sailboats docked for the evening. The last clamor of tourists paused for a look at the sunset over the lake.

What the hell is the matter with you? was the last question he'd asked her. It had taken her two days to return the message. She was on vacation without him because Jim didn't want to be in a cabin in the middle of nowhere. She'd talked him into going with her once. The solitude was too much for him. She'd gathered firewood, waded into the water holding her pant legs up. Took pictures. And at night, she slept like an infant while Jim lay awake, staring into the darkness, bored, her pleasure in the place foreign and baffling. He punished her by leaving a day early. "I've got better things to do," he'd said.

He remembered her standing on the dirt road, in a pair of old shorts and messy hair, watching him drive away, and he was ashamed.

He couldn't stop imagining her last minutes. Even in his room, with his eyes open, he saw her as she left the path, one of many paths that started at cabins and wound through the pines to the cliffs and the lake below them. With his eyes open, he watched as the bear picked up speed.

To move quickly on that root-bound ground would have been treacherous, and Gwen would have known it and fought to keep herself from falling. She was healthy and fast, but it wouldn't have mattered, not there.

Jim turned the television on.

It had been two weeks, the hotel clerk reminded him. He paid her and returned to the woods, rifle in hand, where he would sit or stand until the sun was overhead, as he had each day he'd been in Olagam. It would be all he could do before exhaustion forced him back to town.

He couldn't focus, couldn't stop sweating even as the breeze turned cooler.

The crackle of a twig caused him to stand too quickly and bang the rifle against a tree, his eyes darting through some nearby brush that moved toward him as if pushed by a low blowing wind. Jim's heart pounded. He lifted and cocked the gun, putting his hands where he thought they should go, pointing, pulling the trigger.

The eyes of a raccoon, badly injured but still alive, met Jim's. As fast as he could manage it, he shot again. His hands shook. Gwen would have cried.

Gwen, who in his mind was still in the forest, running, panting, her face blank with fear, eyes piercing the ground as she ran, desperate not to fall, unable to look up to search for a branch low enough to climb.

The bear grunted out his breath as his legs propelled him forward, sure of his footing, used to running on roots and rock. He gave her a playful swat, knocked the breath out of her, and she froze, felt his heart and breath and muscles as he sniffed, drooled on her skin. The massive claw fell, ripped her clothes as if they were made of paper. Impossibly strong, he rolled her, shoved her through the trees toward the water, a last swing belting her into the trunk of a pine hanging in a curve over the cliff edge, its roots clutching the nearby rocks to stay upright. Below her tender, dangling ankle was the rocky shore, the roar of its waves as ferocious as a bear's blow.

The sound of it filled Jim's ears, made his knees clutch. It was what Gwen had heard.

When she was limp, the bear had gone. She hadn't been cut. She hadn't been bitten. She was as pale and beautiful as she had always been. Jim heard the click of a camera and turned to get away from it, groping his way through the trees with his hands and feet until he was outside the woods, where the afternoon was still bright. Clouds made shadows on the road as they passed, low slung and white, traveling in tandem with the wind, toward town and away from the raccoon, struggling to pick itself up on a bed of pine needles, a bullet searing its middle. He drove until he came to the lake, where he and Gwen had stood, watching the shimmer in the sunlight. She'd taken pictures of the water.

Jim told her it was pointless. "There are a hundred postcards in the shops with the same picture on them, and probably better."

"But I didn't take those," she'd said quietly.

And all the years after, she traveled alone.

Jim got out of the car and pushed himself toward the shoreline. There was no one on the beach to watch him crouch awkwardly to keep from falling down the grassy hill. He lifted a pant leg and put a foot in the water, his print dark and heavy as the wave receded.

How they had ignored each other, even as age began to lap at their feet. They'd made a habit of it, for days, or weeks, and the weeks had become a decade.

He saw her in snapshots, all of them old: Gwen in a summer dress, waiting for a bus in the city, Gwen raking leaves in the yard of their first house. And then came a great vacuum in which there were no more pictures, between then and today when all of it was suddenly past, and there was only her body, bruised and tangled in the wind-carved trunk of a tree, her last day spoiled and no chance for anything anymore. He knew nothing of her now except the parts he'd broken, with word or deed or just contempt, long before the bear had broken her neck.

Jim turned to go and picked up his shoes, the imprint they left in the sand as faint as the drawings his wife had made with a stick in the dirt in front of the cabin.

He climbed the hill back to the car. On the seat next to him was the green bag, the name of the mercantile in white script along its front. He closed his fingers around the lump of brown paper and pulled it from the bag. He unwrapped it, unfolding each crease as he rolled it in his palm.

Olagam said an etching in its base. The bear's demeanor was benign, his mouth opened to speak—not roar—nose lifted as if sniffing at a breeze. Thin, scruffy lines created fur that covered his body except for a pronounced mound like a woman's between its legs. Jim slid his thumb tenderly over the smooth, polished finish.

At the end of the block, a sign pointed toward the freeway, in the rearview mirror the road wound back around the lake and toward the woods. Toward the cabin. He rested his head on the steering wheel, holding the bear tightly in his hand.

JACK-O'-LANTERN

I hear him clunking through the kitchen in his winter boots, even though it's only October. My fifteen-year-old grandson, looking for his marijuana. He used to keep it in a little baggie on top of the cupboards, until I surprised him one day and he jumped, arm darting down, hand rushing to his pocket. I heard his mother's voice that day, whispering to me to take action, forbid him to go, something. But I couldn't make out her words. Instead, I rolled my wheelchair back out of the room, saying nothing. He's honest now, and I tell myself it's better to know what he's doing.

He slams the door so hard the hinges rattle, and the paper jack-o'-lantern flutters out from the refrigerator door. The house is falling apart. But the days go by all the same.

Only a few years ago, Ricki drew pumpkins in school, wore a vampire costume. I tell myself he would have grown out of trick-or-treating even if his mother hadn't died. Would have gotten older. Today, he wears no costume. Jeans. Black t-shirt. An old jacket he bought at Goodwill that he won't let me wash, as if it's meant to be a punishment, or a symbol of the burden he bears.

He didn't get the pot habit from his mother. Sandy didn't do drugs or drink in the bars on the weekends like so many in this town. But she rebelled for a while, got pregnant. People in Mercy Lake gossiped as usual, but most didn't have a leg to stand on, and, when they saw what kind of mother she was, the gossip stopped.

I don't have the heart for mothering now, but here we are, Ricki and I, thrown together with no choice in the matter.

So much change. And I can't help but connect it. Sandy died, and then the town died. Two weeks after her funeral, the lumber mill closed, leaving Mercy Lake with no jobs. High school graduates moved on to bigger towns, and their parents followed to wait down the road in senior apartments for grandkids to make life worth living again. Suddenly, everyone was too far away to come back for a family gathering. Too far away to come for just a day.

That's all it took. Years of backyard picnics. Holidays at this cousin's house or that. Then nothing. It's like a TV show Ricki watches, where suddenly half the people in a town wake up to find the other half gone. The whole series plays out without anyone knowing what the point was. He says I just don't get how weird it would be to lose half the people in your life. The thing is, I do.

He parks me in our tiny screened-in porch, with a blanket and a mixing bowl of candy, a battery-operated plastic pumpkin sitting next to me on a table. There's a real jack-o'-lantern on the picnic table just outside the door, lit with two tea candles. I can just open the screen door with my foot to hold the bowl of candy out.

Ricki leaves as the streetlights come on, walking with his hands in his pockets. He won't wear gloves. None of his friends do.

The first trick-or-treaters are small and timid, the shadow of a parent not far behind, little cold hands coming out from under capes, retreating with a tiny chocolate or other wrapped thing; it's hard to see in the dark. A gentle voice floats out of the darkness, and then the child says thank you.

Something turns over in me. This happens now, for no reason—a feeling of grief so strong it makes me gasp for breath, and then I panic. I can't now. Not now.

The next group rounds the corner.

Nostalgia begins the first time you lose someone, I think. The longing for how things used to be. Most people have moved on by the time it hits them. By the time they miss home badly enough to buy a plane ticket, it's gone. The house they grew up in, the cousins chasing fireflies on the lawn, all gone. Maybe that's the hole Ricki's in. Forced too young into longing, remembering.

The end of Halloween comes quietly, as the minute hand ticks toward the official end time, kids coming slower and farther between until there are no more. What's left is the whoosh of the wind through the leaves, a distant car down the main street.

This grief is fathoms deep, and unrelenting, and the only thing to do is ignore it.

I put the last few pieces of candy in my pocket for later and set the bowl on the porch floor, so I can use both hands to stand and open the door to the kitchen, but, after two hours of sitting, my legs won't stand full up. I reach for the doorknob from my chair.

I try to turn the knob a few times, thinking the first effort was too weak, but I know it's locked. It wouldn't be the first time the door locked when it wasn't supposed to, but it is the first time I'm on the wrong side of it. I wrap the blanket around me. *Calm down*, I think. Wait. Ricki has to come home sometime.

This boy, he's not like any boy I knew, and I thought I'd known them all. When he sits, it's in front of the TV. I don't think he's even paying attention to what he's seeing. Swap out the pot smoking and replace it with card playing, and Ricki's as predictable as an old man.

Sometimes he stares out the window with no expression. Other times, he talks and talks, and I think maybe something's wrong with him.

He's too young. We don't know each other. He can't see me.

But I'm right here. Stuck in a porch. Should have brought a little whiskey. Only a few years ago, Sandy would have shared a glass with me.

The streetlight at the corner pools on the blacktop, leaves a spotlight. If I close my eyes, I can imagine Ricki there in his Halloween costume, twirling in his cape.

The jack-o'-lantern burns outside, and the smell of a backyard campfire reaches into the porch from across the street. I wonder about the faces flickering around it—if they're telling ghost stories, teaching a small boy to roast a marshmallow.

I sleep on and off, until I hear Ricki's voice outside and open my mouth to call to him, but there is another voice, maybe Leonard. I lean forward, strain to hear. I hope Ricki won't bring him inside. I don't want his friend to know I've spent hours on the porch. I can't bring myself to speak, though I know the longer I keep quiet, the stranger it will be when they open the door to find me here. Like I've been eavesdropping.

They're laughing. I can smell cigarette smoke and pot, too.

"Your grandma asleep?"

"I guess. Past her bedtime."

"What's her bedtime, seven o'clock? Hey, your pumpkin's still burning. Did you carve this, little Ricki, huh? Let's see it. Hey, did you hear that? Ambulance. Over by Post Street. Remember that movie where the girl gets rescued and the ambulance comes and the killer's riding underneath? Let's have a campfire."

"Kind of late."

"What are you, your grandma now?"

"I don't think we have any wood anyway. I used it last week to burn some leaves."

"You're not supposed to burn leaves, are you? No. You know my dad's the fire chief. He knows this stuff. You can't burn anything within the village limits."

"Then how can we have a campfire?"

"That's different, that's just wood. I mean like, you can't burn stuff to get rid of it."

Ricki laughs. "You're stoned, asshole."

"Maybe."

"Give me that back."

Silence. Then a cough.

"House is pretty dark, Ricki. What if she's dead? She could be turning into a zombie right now."

"Can't you shut up?"

"But what if she was? Dead I mean. Then what?"

"I wish," Ricki says.

I hear it, and gasp, and put my hand over my mouth. At first, I'm afraid of what it could mean.

"Be great to live alone, wouldn't it? 'Cept for cooking. I'd hate to cook."

"Not like she cooks anyway. Just stuff out of a box," says Ricki.

I didn't think he noticed. I put food on the table that's barely a meal, with no care or attention. It's as though I can't see him, don't know him.

"Let's make this pumpkin look like your grandma," says Leonard. He blows out the tea lights and turns the uncarved side toward himself.

"Whatever makes you happy."

"Come on. You got a knife?"

"Just a jackknife."

"This is dull. It's not going to make an eyebrow. That's delicate work. I need something else."

"That's all I have."

"Go in and get something."

"No," says Ricki. "She'll wake up. Use what you have."

"Well, it's a challenge, but I do believe I'm up to it. What about her glasses? You got to give her glasses, or she won't be able to see. How old should I make her?"

"I don't know," Ricki says, "eighty-something, I guess. Whatever. Where's the joint?"

"Here. I'm going to make some wrinkles. If I just cut out little microscopic pieces, there, see? Man, that's fucking fantastic, Ricki, look."

"Pretty good."

"Pretty good, huh? Admit it."

"I just said it, asshole."

"What about the glasses? Find me something for glasses. What's in the garden shed?"

"It's open. Look for yourself."

"Come on, Grandma, let's—"

I hear the pumpkin splat on the sidewalk.

"Shit! I dropped her! I smashed your grandma's head in."

Ricki laughs again, and pretty soon they're both laughing.

I lean my head against the back of my chair. Close my eyes, as if I am sleeping. It will be worse if they know I heard them.

It's the longest twenty minutes of the night. And the embarrassment of being stuck is overshadowed by the more important fact, which is that I've made no home for him. I know that now.

I try to calm myself, but, when he comes in, it's so sudden.

"What are you doing here?" Ricki sounds accusing.

"Oh! You woke me up. I must have fallen asleep. I got stuck here, legs just gave out and I couldn't get back into the house."

I don't want Ricky to see me cry. Nobody wants to see an old lady cry.

"This is what happens when you get old." I try out a laugh. "If you just pull me back, I can get myself to bed."

I can't expect him to care, and that hurts more than anything. He yanks the chair over the threshold.

"Where?"

"This is fine, I can manage from here."

He pushes me to my room.

"Ricki—"

"I'm going back out." He closes the door behind me.

I wheel to the bed and get out of my chair slowly, legs working a little better, and stand with my arms on the windowsill.

From my bedroom window, I see the neighbor's pumpkin, still burning, the leaves rustling past it, and I cry now. For our broken jack-o'-lantern. Could everything really be a failure? Even the good memories seem ruined by loss. I open the window and stand in the autumn chill; maybe I'll stand until the cold chills the self-pity out of me.

I get back in the chair and roll out into the hall, listen.

There are school books on his unmade bed. On the desk, a posed picture. Ricki is smiling, his mother's hand easy on his shoulder. She wears a green sweater; her brown hair is freshly brushed. She was pretty, my daughter. Ricki is eleven in the picture, happy even without a father. Before she died, she built a normal kind of life, dinners together and trips for school clothes in the fall. Daily chores, structure. If Sandy had lived, our days would be different. Instead, here's her son, wandering around as if he can't place himself in the world. But that's my fault, too. I see it now.

I roll into the kitchen and put a sandwich together, and back to the living room, turn on the lights to brighten it up. Lamps next to the couch, the orange and black lights draped across our windows. The TV.

Sometime after midnight, he comes home, reeking of beer and cigarettes.

For a few seconds, he stares at me, waiting for me to ask.

"Have you been drinking?"

"Leave me alone." He reaches for the candy dish.

"Are you hungry? I made you a sandwich. But I promise you, Ricki, you'll have hot meals now. I'll make the meatloaf your mom made for you."

He ignores me.

"Ricki." I touch his arm. "You must hate living here. I don't blame you."

He's still quiet.

"I'm sorry. I was so busy grieving your mother I forgot you lost her, too. I know I can't replace her. But I can do better."

I take off my glasses to pat at my eyes. Embarrassed. I cough, put my hand up to my throat.

"Leonard broke your jack-o'-lantern."

"I know," I say, and laugh. "I heard."

He gently takes the glasses from my lap and wipes them on his black t-shirt, and carefully hands them back.

PICNIC

We packed up the car on a day full of possibilities and traveled past the summer's landmarks: the big Styrofoam ice cream cone in front of the market, the lake and its canoe rentals, and finally Mr. Deer's Indian Trading Post on County T, where the merchandise was thinning and not being replaced. Soon he'd be too old to sell any more moccasins, but today, on this strangely warm day for mid-October, he would do business. And I would be stuck at a family picnic, wearing a skirt instead of shorts. All afternoon. Longer if they brought out the poker chips.

I scowled.

"Ellie! Help me get the stuff out of the car," my mother yelled and opened the trunk. "Take these," she said, handing me a stack of paper plates with salt and pepper shakers balanced on top. "Watch what you're doing."

I picked up the saltshaker I'd dropped. Someone patted my head on the way past as though I were five years old. I scowled.

Picnic tables full of food. Cousin Gaylord with a can of beer, already talking too loudly. Uncle Pat at the grill. Candace rushing after her spoiled kids as they ran in and out of the house.

Same as always.

Except for the strangers. A couple, and a girl. Sitting at the edge of the gathering in lawn chairs.

"Who is that?"

"Don't stare. They're staying at the cabin down by the river." Mom lowered her voice. "They just lost their son."

"What do you mean? He died?"

"Shh. Don't say anything."

The girl's name was Hannah, Mom said. She was sixteen. Her brother had been my age.

Her skin was clear and soft. She wore a plain summer blouse and shorts. I caught sight of myself in the door to the house. Clumsy, chubby, and a little poor, if my clothes were any indication.

Hannah. Even her name was perfect. Her hair was thick and dark, starkly framed by the trunks of the white birches she sat under.

I decided against a second helping of potato salad and wished I'd worn earrings in my newly pierced ears.

She probably had lots of friends and a room without stuffed animals on the bed.

And her brother had died.

This was new territory. Terrible, sad. Mysterious. I was sure it must make her different, that I would see signs if I looked closely enough, but I wouldn't have known if I hadn't been told.

I'd never known anyone who died, except for my grandmother, but she'd been a ghost long before, coming out of the too-bright nursing home to sit in the shadows of our holidays, pinching my cheek on the way to the graveyard. At least that's what she'd said.

I tried not to stare and got up to get dessert, knowing I shouldn't. There was apple pie, easily avoided. And a layer cake with fluffy coconut frosting, not so easy.

"Hannah," she said and put her hand out for a shake.

What kind of teenager shakes hands? I shook it. "Ellen," I said.

"The cake's good," she said. "Do you live around here?"

I cut a slice for myself, trying to match the size she'd taken.

"Few miles," I said, nodding my head west. "This is my aunt and uncle's house."

"Oh. How come I've never seen you here?"

"We don't come out much," I said.

"Why not?"

"I don't know," I said, because I didn't.

"Oh."

She looked around the gathering, played with her fork.

"I have a camera," I said.

"You do?" She smiled.

My parents wouldn't let me have a phone. "I could show you," I said. "It's in my backpack." I waited.

"Sure."

I let her flip through the pictures on my camera herself. I hated when people showed me their pictures, dictating each one as if I had no imagination of my own. Most pictures don't need an explanation. Still, it's hard not to explain why you took them and why they aren't as good as you knew they could be.

Seconds went by as her ringed hands held my little camera and flipped from one to the next.

"Are you sixteen?" I asked.

She smiled. "How did you know?"

I shrugged. "My mom said."

"I like this one." She showed me a picture of our house, white below a dark-blue storm cloud, with the streetlights coming on even in the afternoon.

I felt a smile coming and tried to cover it by looking away.

"And this one, too," she said.

The woods at sunset, leaves glowing red against a golden cornfield.

"Do you have a car?" I asked.

"No. I drive my parents' car sometimes. They let me drive part of the way here. I only have my temps. You're good at taking pictures," she said.

"Really?"

"Yes, really pretty."

"I like to take them," I said. "I got the camera for my birthday last year. There's not much to do around here."

"What are you going to do with them?"

I shrugged.

"You could print them. Give them to people as presents."

I looked at the camera. And back at Hannah.

As soon as I got home I would find earrings to wear and braid my hair the way she did, in one long braid starting at one side and ending on the other, hanging down over her left shoulder.

Cousin Gaylord was getting drunk, standing off to the side in his own world. I knew Hannah saw him too, and I was embarrassed.

"You want to get out of here? Take a walk?"

I told my mother I was going with Hannah. She put a finger to her lips to remind me not to talk about her brother.

We walked through the campground that sat next to the river. There was a little shop where my uncle tied fishing flies that looked like jewelry, and an ancient soda machine that only held Orange Crush in glass bottles.

Hannah called it hiking. She showed me the garage where her family lived. They'd hung curtains to separate the cots from each other and the makeshift kitchen from the cots. Next to the garage was the foundation for the cabin her parents would one day call home. We peered in the windows of the yellow peeling cottage where an old couple named Otto and Erse had lived before they died the summer before. From there, the trail led into woods, thicker and darker than the forest we'd left. The gurgling sound of the river faded, disappearing beneath the sound of the wind in the pines.

"I brought provisions," she said, and laughed at my surprise. She lifted a Ziploc bag of potato chips out of the bag she'd slung over her shoulder. "Let's pretend we're the last people on earth!"

I knew she was trying to entertain me. Had she been alone, I doubt she'd have been playing childish games. But from where we stood, she might have been right. There were pockets in the woods, of darkness and of light, each drawing us forward to see the next and the next. The forest was like a house, not a regular house where people lived, but one without limits. A house with no work to it. Rooms upon rooms for all your thoughts, that expanded as you needed it to.

We couldn't imagine anyone else living there.

I followed her long, bare legs deeper into the woods. She wore hiking boots, and, unlike my sneakers that slid off everything, her boots trod over boulders and branches as though they had fingers to grip them with.

She looked back at me and urged me on into the farthest reaches of the unknown.

"Another planet?" I asked.

"No, I think another country," she said.

"What do you think it's called?"

"I don't know," she said. "Let's come up with something."

"Well, it's got lots of rooms."

"Yes," she said, "it does."

"It's like a mansion," I said.

"A mansion no one else knows about. Why do you think they haven't found it?"

"Because they can't see it, maybe. Only we can," I said.

"Why?"

"Because we have the gift?" I asked.

"Maybe it was the strawberries that gave it to us. I thought they tasted a little different, didn't you?"

"They did," I said, "and no one else ate them."

We walked on. I'd never come this far before. I bet she had though. I bet she had lots of experiences I hadn't. There were so many things I wanted to ask her.

"How come your brother died?" I blurted.

She looked at me and shook her head before walking on.

I wanted to take it back. My mother would be mad, and Hannah had gone quiet. I'd ruined everything.

She walked faster, and I skipped a few times to catch up.

The afternoon was cooling down. I could feel the change on my neck and my legs. Ahead of me, Hannah's shadow had darkened and faded as the sun turned into partial clouds, had become dulled and rich.

"Let's sit over there on that rock," she said.

We sat on a boulder big enough for two. Our feet were almost straight out, our thighs touching.

The coolness had quieted her. She was thinking her own thoughts, kneading stray strands back into her braid.

I didn't want to lose her.

"Let's listen for signs of other life," I said, pretending our silence was part of the game.

She nodded.

I pretended that life was never dull, and that I was never lonely or worried; easy, because, at that moment, I didn't feel that way and it was a relief.

We heard the throaty squabble of a squirrel in a tree overhead. Leaves picked up and pirouetted and dropped again. It was a good forest, widely spaced pines, not a lot of undergrowth. You could see a long way through it, and still it went on, as much mystery as any forest. Sometimes at night when I was going to sleep, I designed a house with all the rooms just as I wanted them. That's what this wood was like, as if someone had gone to sleep thinking of it, and then come and planted it just that way.

The sky was a color you wouldn't believe if it were painted, scary-movie layers of dark blue, black, and bulbous cumulus building above us like walls were going up.

"Take a picture," she said.

We looked at it on the camera's screen.

"It seems the true nature of clouds cannot be captured on film," I said, repeating something I'd read.

She laughed out loud and slapped me on the back. "You've got that right, professor."

Happy.

"It's going to rain," I said.

In a yard through the woods, our families would be standing, looking up, hurrying dishes into the kitchen, wondering where we'd gone.

And then what? Then the day would become ordinary again.

"Civilization," I said.

"I know what you mean," she said.

We felt one drop and another, and more until we had to acknowledge it.

A breeze, a drop.

Thunder.

"Do you think it's the end of the world?" I asked.

"Yes," she whispered.

I turned to look at her and saw that there was a tear on her cheek. The game seemed silly now.

I jumped off the boulder and put my hand out for her.

I led the way, looking back to check on her from time to time. We passed all our checkpoints. I stopped to tap each one and look back, but she didn't tap.

At Otto and Erse's, the clouds were dark in the windows, the yellow of their cabin glowing in the storm-colored air, the grass greener.

"Listen," I said, "we're at the river again."

There was the sound of our feet shuffling, thonking gently where there was only a worn dirt path.

We passed her temporary home and pulled ourselves through the tall grass at the perimeter of the campground, past the handful of tents, and came at last to where we could see the peak of my uncle's roof. It was quiet. I wondered if they'd all eaten strawberries since we'd left and were now taking the same journey we had, or had gone inside to wait out the rain.

Our faces were wet, clothes getting damp. She stopped. I stopped.

"You have some makeup here," I said and gestured to my eyes.

She reached up and wiped at her mascara.

We emerged into the backyard, where the adults were covering dishes and moving them inside, a few at a time. I picked up the bowl of fruit and held it out to her.

"Strawberry," I whispered.

"To the mansion," said Hannah, and touched her berry to mine.

Later, in the car on the way home, I missed her, as though I'd known her for years. I imagined her, lying on the little cot as the rain battered the roof of the makeshift cabin, her parents looking out into the dark woods wondering where everyone had gone, and why they'd taken their son with them. I imagined her closing her eyes, thinking of our walk. For a second I could feel her strong and sure, taking me with her on her travels. I imagined her as a cloud full of electricity, attached to a tether whose end I held.

SMALL INJURIES

Kurt's raging again, this time against a shoe left in the middle of the floor. I've developed a sensitivity to his yelling, like an allergy, a reaction that worsens with every ingestion of the wrong drug, the wrong berry, a peanut.

Outside, we have a flower garden, a small forest, and a pond bordered by a swamp through which I can row. This morning I found a body there. A woman, floating in a dense thicket of reeds. She was dead, I knew it. I dug my oar into the bottom of the pond, to stop myself from drifting closer. From ten feet away, her injury—if there was one—was not visible. She wore a sweat suit, pale blue. Her feet were clad in white socks, toes floating above the water. I rowed back to shore and pulled the rowboat sloppily onto the grass.

"Kurt!"

"What!" he shouted from the open kitchen window.

It was strange to shout "I found a body!" on the quiet autumn day.

He came out, open jacket flapping around his thin frame, limping and grumbling, head snapping left and right as he took in the lawn.

"What are you talking about? Where?"

"Out there. In those reeds on the far side."

He squinted. "I don't see anything."

"You can't see it from here. We have to take the boat."

"Great," he said. Kurt didn't like boats. Or water.

We got close enough to see the sweat suit, and he stopped rowing, just as I had.

"Jesus Christ! Did you call the police?" he asked.

"With what? My shoe phone? Not like I take my cell in the boat."

"Great," he said, digging his oar in the muck. "You have to call the police."

In spring, we'd found an injured squirrel at the base of the maple tree, legs broken, dragging itself in an awful death crawl along the grass. I had been the one to scoop it gently onto a shovel, while Kurt, cursing, went to the closet for a shoebox. I had been the one to lift the little creature into the box, holding it on my lap in the car while Kurt drove us to the Humane Society.

I glanced back at the body. This was no squirrel.

"Goddammit!" he said, so loud I jumped. Anxiety tied little knots in my stomach, the way it always did when something had to be dealt with. First and foremost, I would have to deal with Kurt.

"What's the problem? What's the fucking problem?" I let my oars dangle and turned around.

He leaned toward me, glaring as if the whole thing were my fault.

"They're not just going to come and take her away and be done with it. Think about it. Don't you think it looks a little funny that we have a dead person in our pond?"

"Who cares how it looks? I'm sure it won't take them long to figure out it has nothing to do with us."

"Really? It happened on our property. That makes it our problem."

"Rude of her to die on our property."

"That's not what I meant."

I turned the boat back toward the body. Took a long breath.

"Do you recognize her?" I asked. "She must be from around here."
Kurt shook his head.

"You didn't even look! You know more people here than I do," I said.

Not that he talked to any of them. But since he'd been on disability, he was the one who shopped and ran errands in the little village of Mercy Lake, while I drove twenty miles to the city to work.

Two years ago, he'd fallen from a front loader and smashed his hip. At first, he'd been cheerful. Glad to be off work. He hobbled behind me on crutches, chatting while I did the chores he used to do: clearing out fallen limbs after a windstorm, replacing gutter spouts, directing me as I worked. But the hip didn't heal properly. Pride kept him from rehab with men twice his age, and the limp he had after surgery seemed permanent. One day, when I turned to remark about a loose gutter, I found he'd gone inside, and no amount of good weather would bring him back out.

Instead, he watched television, tired of it, kept watching. His rants grew and festered, exploded, remitted and festered again. There must be a residue from these outbursts, a scar that leaves a trail on the consciousness at large. Everything leaves a trail, even in the water.

I rowed back to shore, harder this time with Kurt's weight in the back, and pulled the little boat onto the bank while he stormed off. I went inside and grabbed my cell phone from the kitchen counter. He poured himself a drink.

"That's a little dramatic, isn't it?" I asked.

A woman's voice answered.

"I found a body," I said, "in my pond."

"Oh! Hold on a minute."

A man's voice answered. I repeated the story. He took my address.

I covered the receiver with my hand. "Now is not a good time to drink."

"Christ," he said, and took his drink into the kitchen.

Ronny Messer, Mercy Lake's only cop, arrived twenty minutes later. I took him out in the rowboat while Kurt waited on shore, arms folded, scowling. He looked like a suspect. But that was how he always looked. Fists clenched, red-faced, ready to defend himself.

This time I couldn't avoid seeing her face. Ronny took her arm and pulled her closer, like a buoy. Whatever had caused her death I still couldn't tell. Her expression was one of surprise, wide-eyed, slightly open mouth, but it was clean and unhurt. It was as if she hadn't yet made sense of all her life coming to this one moment.

"That's Poppy Heller!" Ronny unhooked his radio from his belt. "I've got to call this in."

Ronny waited in our living room for a squad from a neighboring town, with the sheriff and another officer in it, and then they went to haul Poppy out.

"They finished the coffee," Kurt shouted from the kitchen.

"I'm going outside," I said.

Kurt had been right. It was a long process. There weren't a lot of dead bodies in Mercy Lake. Certainly none like Poppy Heller, floating face up in a pond.

The cops peered over the side of the boat, gestured at each other, peered again. They rowed back. There was much discussion. The problem seemed to be that they couldn't get her in the boat without getting into the water themselves. The October morning was chilly, the pond cold and waist deep, maybe more.

"Sorry to bother you," Ronny said, walking toward me, "but have you got a rope somewhere?"

Kurt was no longer in the window. I jogged to the door and opened it to yell inside.

"A rope? For what?"

"Can you just get a rope, Kurt?"

A few minutes later, he brought one from the basement. The officers rowed back out and tied it around Poppy's feet. Ronny looped the other end around the bench in the boat. They brought her in like a big fish.

The sheriff approached us.

"You should know," he said and glanced at the other officer, "it looks like Poppy's been shot. There's a hole in her back."

"Christ," Kurt said.

"Wasn't a large caliber—what do you think?"

"Well, judging by the size of the wound," said Ronny, "I'd say—"

"I don't want to hear about it," said Kurt, waving.

By then, the officers had explored our pond and the woods around it, and I'd repeated the story to at least half a dozen curious neighbors. As the only cop assigned to Mercy Lake, Ronny's car was always noticed, that is, if it was on the move instead of parked on some back road while he checked his Instagram. The silver sheriff's car with the official insignia on the side, traveling our country road first thing in the morning, had drawn out a group of our neighbors who stood in a little cluster at the edge of the yard, whispering and craning their necks to get a look at a dead person, waving me over to hear the tale.

The cops had taken Kurt aside and asked him the same questions they'd asked me. I could hear the annoyance in his voice when he repeated over and over that he'd been inside, he knew nothing more about it than they did.

"Coroner will have to come and get the body," Ronny told us.

"How long will that take?" Kurt asked.

Ronny shrugged. "Hour or so."

Kurt snorted. "You're just going to leave her there?"

"We can't put her in the squad car, Mr. Lansing."

"We'd better not be suspects here."

"Oh no, I don't think so. You folks just go about your business and, well, maybe make sure the animals don't get at her."

I heard Kurt gasp. He glared at me. I shrugged.

We all looked at Poppy Heller, drying out on the bank.

The rest of the morning passed slowly. Kurt pouted and paced. I tried to go about my business. Both of us kept coming back to the kitchen window.

"I feel like we should do something. Put a blanket over her," I said.

Kurt drove his fingers through his hair, turned away. "This is the last thing I need!" he said.

"The last thing you need? A woman's dead. Dead! She probably has a husband or kids, someone waiting for her. They're going to have a terrible day. Think of somebody else for a change."

I got a blanket from the porch, scratchy with dirt and leaves, and shook it out. In the kitchen window, Kurt stood still, watching, and then was gone.

I knelt down. Her sweatshirt was twisted. I straightened it as well as I could without touching her, though I knew it couldn't be causing her any discomfort. Silly how some things compel you to fix them, no matter how inconsequential. She wore a necklace, a small silver heart on a silver chain. One of a million. Nothing to distinguish her from a thousand other women. She was a human being alone, still visible in the world, but only for a few more hours. I pulled the blanket over her sad, bluing face, at a loss for what more I could do.

We watched as the coroner came and put her on a gurney, bumping it along the side of the house and over the backyard where he'd driven right up alongside Poppy.

She left an indentation on our lawn, a patch of lightly trampled grass. Other than that, the pond was back to normal, though the sky had darkened and a light rain had begun to fall. The backyard seemed emptier than it had been before.

It *was* empty, I told myself, but the seed had been planted, first in my mind—I'd felt it as soon as Poppy was gone. And sometime just before nightfall it occurred to Kurt that whoever had killed Poppy Heller could still be out there. The realization hit him as he put the teapot on the stove and then abruptly went again to the window, craning his neck left and right to see the whole of the back of our property. After supper, he said it out loud.

"They always come back, to see if the body's been found," he said.

It was the first time all day he'd spoken to me without yelling.

From time to time, he got off the couch to open the blinds a crack. At nine o'clock, he called the police and asked if we should be worried.

"Don't worry about it? Are you kidding?"

He snorted.

He limped over to the door and checked it again.

Until his injury, Kurt had worked at the lumber mill. He'd been impossible to live with then, his muscles always sore, hair full of sawdust, hands bruised and full of tiny cuts. I thought the rest would cure him of the anxiety I assumed was job related. But he nursed it like an infant, and, after a brief respite, it was stronger than ever. Even the roofers who'd come in spring learned to avoid him. I could see them tighten whenever he came outside to watch them work, arms folded, pacing back and forth.

"They said we should take notice of any strange cars." He walked to the front door and peered out. Our driveway was long and wound through dense pine forest for a quarter mile before reaching the county highway.

"We're in the middle of nowhere. Any car is strange. Besides, no one could find this house," I said, trying to laugh.

"They already did," said Kurt.

The music on the television increased in volume, a panicked violin pleading as a path was traversed by an unknown walker. A body had been found, this one young and glamorous, wearing nothing but a diaphanous white nightgown. Kurt muted it.

"Yeah, right," Kurt said, snorting. "It's not quite like that, is it?"

"*I* found the body."

"So?"

"So stop acting like someone did it to you."

The clock ticked from the adjacent dining room.

"We could go to a hotel," he said.

"For Christ's sake. No. We're not going to a hotel. At least, I'm not. It could take weeks for them to figure this out."

He wouldn't leave, I knew. Not if I didn't. In the meantime, he would take all the air out of the room. As for me, I couldn't even decide if I was scared or upset, because Kurt did all the emoting for both of us. There was no room for anyone else.

Our bedroom was at the back of the house, its windows shrouded by a large pine we'd meant to take down. It was full of shadows at night made by a light we left on over the nearby garage. *A killer will come in the front door as surely as he'll come in the bedroom window*, I thought. Fear would not force me out of my bed.

Sleep didn't come. I couldn't stop anticipating a shadow, the sudden appearance of a face at the window.

I settled on the shorter of our couches in the living room and turned the lamps off. Kurt laughed, one laugh, more like an expulsion of air from the other side of the room. I ignored him.

The room was dark except for the television, full of a screaming face with no sound and its reflection in Kurt's glasses. I could feel his eyes on me.

"They made tire tracks all over the yard," he said in the darkness. "Deep ones. With that hearse."

I picked up the remote and turned the channel.

"Here," he said. "In *our* yard."

I would have to plant some grass, I thought.

"It's worse if it's a total stranger," he said. "The closer the relationship, the closer the shot. That's what they say. This wasn't a close shot."

"For Christ's sake, it was probably an accident."

"It's not hunting season," he said.

I thought about that. "Did you lock the door?"

Sure enough, he checked again.

At dawn, the couch was empty except for a rumpled blanket and pillow. I found Kurt in the kitchen, rifling through drawers, slamming each one as he finished. There were dark circles under his eyes.

"What are you looking for?"

"Bullets. We have one bullet. One. That makes a lot of sense, doesn't it?" The rifle that had belonged to my father was leaning against the cupboards.

"For what?"

"Isn't that obvious?" He slammed another drawer.

"Stop it!" I said and put a hand on his arm. "Kurt, come on. What are you going to do, shoot somebody? This is ridiculous. Whoever killed Poppy is long gone," I said.

He pulled his arm away.

"You don't know that." He sat down at the table with the gun and got the bullet out of his shirt pocket and loaded it into the gun.

"Get that thing off the table."

He ignored me.

"I mean it. I don't want a loaded gun in the house. Take it outside!"

He grabbed the weapon and yanked on his jacket. The screen door banged shut behind him.

In the bathroom in my t-shirt and socks, I spread the bath mat on the floor, poured in some bubbles, and started the tap. Just before getting in, I reached for the mirrored door in the medicine cabinet and opened it. Press, twist, dump a little pill in my hand. The pills were Kurt's, and I was doing it out of spite, but soon enough the effects of the painkiller would make me resolve to be kinder. I closed the cabinet and saw myself. Brown hair, brown eyes, a few wrinkles just begun at their corners. Nothing to distinguish me from a thousand other women.

The house was quiet. I strained to listen as a sound came in through the partially open window, a faint, unmistakable sound, shuffling, coughing, mumbling. I opened the blinds.

Kurt was outside, uneven and awkward on the lumpy grass, gathering stray branches with one hand, clutching the gun in the other. A familiar sorrow awakened in my stomach and spread to my heart. I needed the pill, I told myself, to keep my head above water, to make an attempt to be compassionate, one more time.

He dragged a lawn chair out of the shed and sat.

For a few minutes, I tried to relax in the tub, but the image of Poppy wouldn't leave me. I let my feet float in the water and leaned back, until I thought I felt the brush of reeds along my back.

"You can't stand guard forever." I handed him a cup of coffee. "Whoever the killer is, I'm sure he could outlast you." I attempted to laugh.

Kurt scowled.

"Why don't you paint the shed door while you're out here?" I suggested.

"Because it's wet, that's why."

"The door is not wet."

"It's damp outside. Paint doesn't dry in damp air."

He had a point.

"Nobody's going to come to our house, Kurt. This isn't the scene of the crime." I pointed at the pond. "That is." Yet, someone might, said a voice in my head. Someone might think we'd seen whatever had prompted the extinguishment of Poppy Heller. He could be drawn back, invited by the fear and dread that seemed to surround us. Sometimes bad things find you by walking in your own footsteps.

I thought about the painkillers in the bathroom cabinet.

"What exactly do you think you're going to do?"

He sat forward. "Shh. Look. Look!"

"What? I don't see anything."

He was out of the chair, walking slowly, quietly toward the left bank of the pond. I stood, too. Kurt hesitated at the edge of the woods and then went in, gun in hand. He disappeared behind a tangle of brush. It had gotten colder. I zipped my jacket and turned up the collar. Around the pond, what color there was had thinned in the overnight wind, but the woods were dense, and I couldn't see him. Only the twitch and wave of branches here and there signaled his progress to the back of the property. Ridiculous, I thought. And then I heard a shot.

I threw the mug and ran. I stopped short. A shape lay on the ground. A deer on its side, panting, alert enough to kick out at the air. On his knees, Kurt put a hand on the ground to steady himself as he bent forward to look closer. He spun around when he heard me.

"I hit him. I saw something moving, and I just—I hit him."

The animal kicked and panted, trying to propel itself upward by jerking its head.

"Stupid! Look what you did!" I pushed him backward. He lost his balance and fell. I didn't care. "You've got to kill him. He's suffering!"

"I don't have any more bullets!"

"You can't leave him like this!"

He stumbled around the animal, looking around at the forest as if it could help him end the sound of the deer's gasping and pretend it never happened.

"What's the matter with you? Are you going to let it suffer? Are you?"

He wouldn't respond.

Brush snapped my cheeks as I ran out of the woods, then across the lawn to the garden shed. Tools hung on hooks, leaned against the walls, and at that moment they were just shapes I couldn't connect to names or uses. I grabbed blindly, a shovel, something else, and ran back.

"What are you going to do with a goddamn hammer?" Kurt limped a few feet away and turned to look back at me. The deer struggled, its eyes wild, legs kicking. The two of us standing there were prolonging its misery and its panic.

I picked up the shovel and immediately knew it wasn't the right tool. Its handle was long for leverage, its shovel too light. I dropped it and picked up the hammer, thrusting it toward Kurt.

"Kill it! You fucking coward! Kill it!"

Kurt stood taut, barely breathing while the deer continued to pant and wheeze. He made no move toward the hammer.

"Coward!"

The deer's flailing grew more frantic.

I stepped around it, trying to avoid crunching things under my feet, hoping it would die before I had to bring the hammer down on its smooth brown head. How close would I have to be?

"From behind!" Kurt shouted.

I inched closer. It was a mistake. The animal panicked. I lifted the hammer, and it kicked outward, heaving itself toward me, legs flailing. A hoof knocked the air out of me, and I sat, the world a blur.

"Don't move! Don't move!" Kurt yelled.

I heard a loud crack.

When I next opened my eyes, I was traveling on my back, under a gray, featureless sky.

Kurt bent over me, blocking out the sun.

"I killed it," he said, "with the hammer."

"Too late," I said. I felt myself slide into the back of the ambulance.

He kept all the lights on in the house, all the time.

"Here," he said, and handed me a bowl of soup. "It'll be dark soon."

The local warden had removed the deer, Kurt said, more efficiently than the police had removed Poppy, whose killer was still at large.

Kurt hovered, brought an extra blanket to the couch where I was recovering from bruised lungs and broken ribs. He'd been busy, fixing a bedroom window that didn't close, installing a new light at the back door.

For weeks, he clung to the incident of Poppy as though it was a life raft, and her killer, still unfound, our common purpose. We would work as a team, he said. He would patrol the perimeter; I would watch, listen.

I was certain that our own anxieties, little cruelties toward each other, had spread out, left a trail for a murderer to follow, and that he would find us again. But even we could not summon him, and the nightmare slipped away, leaving only the emptiness it had replaced.

Anytime now, the police would call and tell us it was over. That it had nothing to do with us. And then what? What then? Poppy had died on our property. Her death had changed nothing, and that was more than I could bear.

"You left the rowboat out," Kurt said. "Now it's frozen to the bank of the pond."

"I guess you'll have to move it in spring," I said.

"It'll be ruined by then," he said and banged down his coffee mug.

"I'm sorry," I said. "About everything." I reached out for him, but he jerked away.

The jumbled heap of moving boxes in the living room were all mine, and I was sorry. Sorry that even when I walked out the door for the last time, he'd still be pretending to be mad about the boat.

The doorbell rang.

Poppy's daughter stood at our door. She held out her hand and started to speak, but we knew who she was before she got the words out. She had Poppy's face.

"Lily? Your name is Lily?" Kurt said. I turned my head to give him a warning glance, but he was smiling, and it took me aback. All I could do was stare, until tears began to gather, and then Lily laughed.

She said she'd come to see the last place her mother had inhabited. She wore a bright parka and jeans, standing uncomfortably amidst the boxes and the chill in the room, hands in her coat pockets.

"Can't really see much right now," said Kurt. "Ice."

"That's okay."

Kurt put on his jacket.

"I'd like to go alone, if you don't mind. I'll just be a minute."

He showed her out the side door. For a while, we watched together, almost touching, almost. At first, she stood still, head down. She couldn't have known her mother had lain where she now stood, but she looked so long I wondered if somehow Poppy's presence lingered there. Then, just as we had weeks before, she lifted her gaze to the bony trees at the far edge and folded her arms around herself. I could almost feel her shiver.

RUNNING WITH MRS. GINGERLAKE

Some people say sex is the ultimate awareness of being alive. I disagree. Running is. It starts with putting on the clothes, the running clothes. Loose, something a body can move in as it was meant to. Human beings were not meant to sit.

Next comes the closing of the door, keys in pocket, double-checking to make sure. The slow, self-conscious beginning when you lift one foot higher and then the next, and propel yourself a few inches over the ground. There is always a moment when you think of turning back, back to the couch, the yard, the car. A foot leaps and comes down and makes contact, and your heart stirs. Sweat begins to moisten clothing. And then you are filled with wonder that you can do this, and after a mile the body remembers and embraces the action.

Before the accident, my limbs moved easily—there was no pain, no stiffness. Sometimes when my heartbeat felt strong, I felt capable as an animal, part of the world, surefooted through the woods and over the fields. Not weightless, but in command of my weight. Plans and worries cleared away to make room for oxygen. Thoughts passed by without stress, distracted as I was by trees or deer or clumps of flowers.

This was what I'd valued above everything—the feeling of invincibility that running gave me. What I longed for now.

Which left me in a pickle, since an accident had left me a paraplegic. At thirty-five, the thought of spending the rest of my life in a wheelchair, captive, was as horrifying as the memory of Beck staring at me from the passenger seat. But I was the lucky one. Beck was dead.

Alone in my living room, I poured another drink. It is a uniquely human thing to want the one thing you can't have. At least, I assume that a dog does not long to walk on two legs, or dream of being a cat. No matter how much I drank, there remained that one desire, not to think, but to run. To move. To be free.

For months in the hospital, there were tests, and hope, and then none. This was followed by an attempt at rehabilitation, which I remember as a big white smear of pain. In hindsight, the hospital was not without advantage. It was a foreign land, a place so separate from my life that it seemed possible that, when I left, I would also leave behind the accident and all it meant. Everything would be normal. The foyer with its jumble of jackets and shoes, the kitchen table we'd used more for projects than meals, and Beck, my wife of ten years, in a t-shirt and leggings, deadheading flowers in the backyard. Waiting for me to call out "I'm home."

I was not prepared for the quiet. A spot had been cleared in the living room for my chair, and I sat there that first day, in a space formerly occupied by an end table, awaiting the departure of the nurse and the arrival of a friend who would fill the gaps between caregivers for a few weeks until I could find someone full-time.

No mugs sat drying on the drainboard, no shirts hung on chair backs, no socks balled up among the dust bunnies under the couch. Clean, impersonal. The signs of our life together, or any life in the house, were gone, because the signs of Beck were gone, all but some mail on the kitchen counter addressed to Rebecca Lynn Wilder.

Friends assured me that things had been *put away, Allan, not stolen or thrown out.* The past had gone to storage. I wanted it back, that still life of us in one moment, before everything went to shit. They'd made it impossible.

There were dainty ticking sounds in the house I'd never noticed. Creaks the floor made when I wheeled over them, slowly, still not used to propelling myself and the hospital-issued, forty-five-pound wheelchair from room to room in a house with floors not meant for gliding. Soon I would have an electric version.

My fellow scientists visited, too. Logical people, accustomed to spending the day in laboratories and classrooms, and ill-equipped for human tragedy. I had changed, become a person of mystery. An "other" whose life and experience were so foreign to their own, and dreadful. They looked at me with curiosity, or awe, or wearing the kind of pious face reserved for those who are doing the right thing. My favorite was Milton, a not-so-closeted smoker who stopped to have a few tokes on my porch before knocking.

"Well this sucks, Allan, but you know, you'll be back at work sooner than you think. We can get you set up here. And you know the lab is accessible. I'm getting ahead of myself here, but when you're ready, you know, when you're . . ."

I worried they'd all stop coming, once I had a nurse and it was no longer likely I'd sit there dead for days if someone didn't come.

For the first time, I noticed the columns of dust floating in the sunbeams that came into the living room, settling on the tops of the coffee table, the bookshelf, the television's dead screen. It felt as if I had crossed over to some other realm, an alternative reality on the other side of the mirror, or behind the walls buzzing with afternoon light. I could see Beck and me in the room, sitting on the couch with the big picture window in front of us, the setting sun making our ordinary things look golden and precious. I could hear our voices, feel the weight of the plate in my lap that held a still-sizzling pork chop, buttered carrots, baked potato.

Only a few months earlier, we'd argued about the workings of memory. I said memories were the result of electricity, synaptic flashes—not to be trusted. She, on the other hand, had a theory that the strongest ones were the result of many things happening together to form one perfect second, a magical second that could masquerade as an entire era. This was based on several of her own recollections, like her cousins playing croquet on the lawn, which, after phone calls with said cousins, was determined to be the happenings of only an evening, not entire summers, not years. Neither of you can be sure, I'd said. Twenty years can play tricks on one's mind. And what does it matter anyway? You must keep emotion from tainting your memories. I actually said that. I was ridiculous, back then. But I was also a scientist, my life full of problems and experiments, to the exclusion of all else.

Maybe she was right. The truth might be that once, for a few seconds, I saw Beck outside, standing in the garden, and the news was on, and there was sunlight, and I had food, and I felt so much love.

I couldn't face those rooms, that slant of light. Things began to blur. People came and went, pills were everywhere, in bottles, on end tables, in plastic segmented boxes marked a.m. and p.m., always a stray capsule on the rug in the living room. Our house was built for healthy people who could walk and bend and reach, and it mocked my new two-wheeled lower half. Every ingress and egress was a frustrating and painful task.

The choice was clear. Our house, Beck's and mine, would not be changed. Leaving felt like cowardice. Like running away, but it was the only kind of running I could still do.

At the end of Rocking Horse Road was a cottage, in a clearing surrounded by forest. It was simple. One story, redwood siding. A box with a few rooms inside. At the front was a porch and the only obstacle—three steps—easily solved with a ramp.

Beck would have daydreamed on this porch, I thought, eyes reflecting clouds, coffee cupped between palms, and I would have belittled her for it. Ironically, daydreaming was all I had left. From morning until early evening, when I attempted, though never succeeded, to extinguish myself with brandy, I sat on that porch, staring into the woods, conversing with the ceramic rabbit who'd been there to greet me when I moved in. Alcohol softened the anxiety, dimmed reality. Why? Why all of it? Was there a God? If only I wasn't in the wheelchair, I thought, I could have dealt with the rest.

Part of the reality was that, added to the pills I was taking, I couldn't handle much liquor. I'd become a cheap date. Even one glass of wine made me feel lucky to already be seated.

I don't remember hiring Mrs. Gingerlake. I'm sure I did, or someone did, though sometimes it seems she came with the house, had always been there. She came every morning, passing by the bedroom window, hand lifted in a wave that was half good morning, half go to hell, and then I'd hear the click of the lock in the cottage door.

"How did you sleep, Allan?"

"Okay."

"Boogeyman come?"

"Nope," I said.

"Too bad."

She was middle-aged, slack of cheek, her eyes striking, hair white and always hanging down her back in a long, loose braid. She was strong as an ox, and muscular, aside from a little extra weight around her middle.

A leather cord, at the end of which was a bird with outstretched wings, dangled over me as she gave me my morning bath.

"Can you take that thing off? It's tickling my chest hairs."

She flung it around so that it hung behind her. "You take a lot of maintenance." She glanced around the litter of books and medical equipment in the small bedroom, scrubbed my privates with more vigor than necessary.

"Can't feel a thing," I said.

"Can't blame me for trying."

She helped me into the wheelchair, easy since my weight was mostly bone and loose flesh. Besides, Mrs. Gingerlake was a professional caregiver. A lifetime of lifting people had given her biceps that could crush a man's head.

She was pleasantly ludicrous, accusing me of leaving a mess, for example, on the top shelf of the cupboard, which of course she knew I couldn't reach. She suspected I could move, she said, pretended to be paralyzed so someone would pamper me. It was a relief, not to be pitied and babied.

She pushed me out onto the porch.

"There, now the fire ants will get you."

"You wish," I said, but the cottage door had already slammed.

The wind was distilled through the woods and dust of Rocking Horse Road, landing on my face and neck, as close to intimate touch as I'd experienced in months. I raised my chin, closed my eyes, and let myself miss her. I missed my wife, remembered the feel of her physically near me, her life standing next to mine. I begged a god whose presence I couldn't feel to put her back, wishing so hard, so desperately, it hurt. And crying when it was all for nothing. There was no Beck.

Just the wind.

When it rained, Mrs. Gingerlake parked me close to the cottage under a meager awning and covered my knees with a tarp. Mentally, I walked the perimeter of the lawn, touching each tree as it faded in the early evening to pale gray and loomed up dark once the sun set. I closed my eyes and imagined the lovely uneven ground in the forest. I could smell the musty earth exposed where a squirrel had buried a nut, feel the brush of pine branches across my arms.

Beck was leaving me. She'd announced it in the car, as we were passing in front of the cigar store on Main Street, just as the streetlights were blinking on.

I suppose the fact that I hadn't seen it coming is an indication that I deserved it. Once she said it out loud, it was obvious—she'd been suffering a long time, and I hadn't noticed. Long enough that her decision to leave was firm, final.

The world changed. It was as if someone had erected a circus tent the color of a stormy summer sky. The streetlights became jeweled elephants and fire-eaters, and a truck, barreling toward us on our side of the road, was a lion let out of its cage, running straight at us. There was nowhere to go. On the right was a steep drop-off, a cliff that rose over the lake, so I swerved left. The lion caught Beck in its jaws and crushed her.

At noon, Mrs. Gingerlake brought me in from the porch, stepping past me down the steps and into the grass, calling out, "Allan! Where are you? It's time for lunch. Oh, there you are. I heard the bump of the door."

"Lunch," Allan said.

And the day went on.

When the body is imprisoned, the mind attempts to compensate— it works overtime. I had a mind all right, but it had been trained on problems with answers. It wasn't used to being preoccupied with constant pain, worry, fear, regret, death. Guilt that I'd lived, guilt that I was making no effort to return to research, wallowing in self-pity. After all, I was still alive. I could smell the rain, shiver in the balding October soon to come. I could have Mrs. Gingerlake bring me a cup of tea and a blanket. Beck was always talking about the little things in life. How they deserved notice and importance. Now, I understood what she meant by little things. I was pretty sure that one day they'd kill me.

Out of desperation, I tried to entertain myself with my mind, first an attempt to meditate, using as my guide a little book on transcendental meditation, a remnant of the seventies also left by previous owners. I had no better ideas. The book suggested that, with a clear, empty mind, a person could find peace. Total bullshit. Still, maybe under the repetitive doomsday chatter, cultural implants, TV commercials, there was really something more.

How deep did I go? I tried and tried to clear space in my mind for a great epiphanic peace to move in, to no avail. Depression and self-pity had become friends, leaning on my shoulders with their heavy, comforting weight. The contemptible hobby of self-reflection was the last available to me. Beck would have said it served me right.

If my mind was a chaotic and messy landscape, meditation provided nothing more than a flimsy rake, turning over the shallowest, most obvious layers. To get to the bottom of myself I needed more than a rake. I needed heavy equipment, and for that I began to search.

Mrs. Gingerlake perused the stacks of books I ordered online, even selecting titles for me. I'd become a fan of a book that had weight, not pixels, books I could carry on my lap as I rolled from room to room, though I had to review more recent research only online.

She was intuitive, I'll give her that. She brought advice on living up to my potential. Recovering from grief. Zen masters from Cleveland, handsome psychiatrists. Happy places, inner peace, self-actualization, individuation. Bullshit. Macrobiotics. Christ, Krishna, Buddha. Mind control. That was interesting.

Looking back, I swear I remember a little tinkling bell sounding as I retrieved from the latest stack a book called *Moving Objects with Thought: Telekinesis for Everyone*, and thinking *close, but not right. Not yet.*

I wondered if the drugs I took would affect my efforts to try the exercises. Which would muddy the waters more: despair, pain, or the pharmaceuticals that smothered them? I tried to move the brandy bottle from one side of the table to the other. Waited. Giggled. Bullshit. It wasn't terribly disappointing. After all, I had no idea what I wanted to accomplish, except that bending a spoon to impress people at parties wasn't it.

And then Mrs. Gingerlake set before me a title that made my spine tingle, though of course, that was probably imaginary. *Times Three*, written by one Dr. Mann Friess. It was a thick, old book with a faded blue cover, its title so preposterously small I thought it must be embarrassed. Chapter headings included "Beyond Meditation," "Spiritual Travel," "Astral Projection." Bullshit, I said to myself, but more quietly this time, because the bell was ringing again, only louder. So loud I was sure she could hear it from inside the house. I started reading.

I read the last, long chapter and reread it, day after day, the breeze curling the edges of the pages.

"Glad to see you're enjoying that, Allan," said Mrs. Gingerlake one morning, and sat down on the top step next to my wheelchair, a glass of lemonade next to her, and lit a cigarette.

"Yes," I said, and thought, *It's fantastic, and maybe, just maybe, it's going to mean a whole new world for me.* "It's teaching me how to control *The Help*."

She didn't laugh. "I read it," she said.

"Really?"

"Long time ago. Looks like that birch is dying," she said.

Hope is a fool's game, my mother had said, to which Beck replied under her breath that my mother wouldn't recognize hope if it sat at her dinner table wearing a tuxedo.

Where had I stood on hope? It hadn't been something I needed. My days were full of projects. I had a nice wife and house. I ran every morning, rain or shine, and one day ran into the next like it should. I cultivated useful thoughts. Abstract concepts like love, dreams, happiness? Well, they existed, or they didn't. It was a waste of time to torture yourself wondering if you had the right amount of them, or what your family had done to leech them out of you. You didn't hope for the future; you worked for it.

I studied. And felt embarrassed. And studied some more. I became curious about the author of *Times Three*. I had to know Mann Friess.

He wasn't easy to find. *Times Three* hadn't exactly been a bestseller.

His voice was deep, a little raspy.

"Dr. Friess? I'm sorry to intrude, I was calling about a book you wrote. My name is Allan. I'm a scientist. Or was."

Why had I said *was*? Wasn't I only on leave?

There was a little laugh at the other end.

"Excuse me?"

"Sorry. I'm not laughing at you. It's just that it's such an old book. No one has contacted me about it in years. One would have thought I'd have quacks crawling down my driveway at all hours."

"I'm not a quack, if you don't mind. Some people might say that you are, actually."

"Don't get defensive. I'm not a quack either. Would I have written six hundred pages on a subject without any evidence for its truth?"

My heart skipped a beat.

"I'm a paraplegic," I said, "and then some. I was in an accident."

"Ah."

"How can this really be possible?"

"How can anything be possible? Scientists"—he snorted—"you place all your trust in the mind, but only as far as your current studies, what your paid projects require. Suspend your disbelief. That won't make it happen, but it will clear the way for you to do what's necessary."

There was a long pause. *Show me*, I wanted to say. Help me. Save me.

"Allan. Try the method I outlined. Keep trying. It's like any scientific experiment. The mind *can* be trained. You know this. You've just never thought of using it in this way. Scientists can be strangely limited. Outrageously so, in fact."

"It seems like some old hippie sort of idea."

"Please. Hippies couldn't have achieved anything like this. This takes discipline. Not crystals. Not pretending. And certainly not pot."

"Are you really telling me you've done it?"

"Call me when you've put some effort into it."

And with that our conversation came to an end.

"Listen, I need a favor," I said.

Mrs. Gingerlake put her hands on her hips.

"Oh?"

A massive bullfrog croaked, and the wind died down at just that moment, as if the trees had dropped their limbs to listen.

"I want to stay out here for the night. After supper you can—"

"All night?" Mrs. Gingerlake put down her lemonade. I tried not to look at *Times Three*. I didn't want her to guess my motives. "You'll get cold, and what if—"

"I can get back inside if I need to. It's hard, but I can do it." I had no idea if this was true. Usually Mrs. Gingerlake left around 8:00 p.m. when my only tasks left were to operate the remote control and try not to drink too much liquid. I wore a diaper at night. I'd long since gotten over feeling self-conscious about it, but why lean into it?

I should have had live-in help, probably, but the thought of letting go of this last bit of solitude was more than I could bear. Uncomfortable as I sometimes was while alone, this remnant of independence was worth it.

It occurred to me that it might be tricky to open a screen door with my left arm and then keep it open while maneuvering into a position to roll over the shallow but worrisome threshold with one good arm and one that only worked part-time. Then again, the worst that could happen was that I'd be stuck outside until Mrs. Gingerlake returned in the morning.

I had experimented several times in the safety of the cottage, but the landscape outside the front window, the pines with their secret dark spaces, beckoned me at night. *I'm trusting my gut, Beck. I'm going outside.*

"You could bring down the old army sleeping bag. It's in the loft. That should be enough to keep me warm," I said.

"I'll think about it," she said.

I didn't like her tone this time. She didn't seem to be kidding.

"Mrs. Gingerlake. I am not a child."

She stopped midway across the porch.

"I know it," she said, and looked back at me. "I'm sorry."

I waved my good hand.

For half an hour, she was in and out with supplies—the sleeping bag, oxygen just in case, a bottle of water—staring at me like I was a puzzle, trying to figure out everything I might need. Before she left for the night, she set down a plate with two sandwiches, pickles, chips.

"Protein," she said. "Hey, you picked a good night. Full moon. Just saw it on the weather." Her keys dangled in her hand. "You want me to stay with you? I could, I'd just have to run home and get a few things."

"No, I do not. I've had quite enough of you for one day," I said.

She turned around.

"We all have our prisons, Allan."

"Rita."

"Sorry."

"It's all right."

"Are you sure you don't want the radio or the TV out here? There's an extension cord—"

"God, no."

"Then I guess I'll take off." She hesitated.

"For crying out loud, what's the difference? In, out, am I going to freeze to death in September? Be eaten by a wild animal?"

"I can dream," she said. "Goodnight, Allan."

She walked to her car, got in, and waved as she drove off.

It was glorious at first, sitting there, outside, alone as night fell. I wondered why I hadn't done it before. Previous attempts at using the method had involved candles in the living room of the cottage, a narrow, paneled room that mirrored the layout of the porch.

The meditation phase of the exercise started slowly. The pines grew black; the stars grew brighter.

It is surprisingly difficult to think of nothing, and that was only the warm-up for this task. In a much-simplified form, the exercise went like this: Empty your mind of thoughts. *Times one.* Focus on walking the mind through a sort of imagined landscape of simple surfaces and "bumpers" like the ones in a pinball machine. *Times two.* Each time you hit a bumper, add one of the concepts or images specifically designed to fire certain neurons as outlined in the final chapters. *Times three.* When you're ready and sufficiently able to keep your mind focused, focus on the place you've chosen to be in previous exercises.

It was hard even for me, and I was, for all practical purposes, arduously trained to focus on a task.

I couldn't help but be aware of the beauty of the night around me. Memories came. Some I enjoyed, some I feared. All of them ended in a wheelchair, and a sense of dread as immediate as a slap.

I cried and worried about stuffing up my nose. Mrs. Gingerlake had forgotten to leave a box of tissues.

To empty my mind, I made myself catalog the shapes of leaves and the ways they determined the sound the wind made as it passed through them. Focus. A noise in the woods gave me a start when I realized it was not the usual deer, but a black bear. I panicked. *Stay calm*, I thought, *it's no problem*. Wild animals are about the chase. I was more like roadkill than viable prey. Eventually, I relaxed, as the bear, bored with trying to find berries on spent bushes, jogged off into the woods, only flashes of his fur visible as he went.

I endured a phantom itch somewhere in the left hip region for longer than usual and checked in on the constant pain in my back to see what it was up to.

Something was dawning in me. An awareness of every little tick and scratch in the woods. It felt like the start of a love, or a cold. It was a yearning so strong I couldn't turn it off even when I wished it would stop. My thoughts accelerated, like too much wine too fast, pushing me toward an unknown I worried about surviving.

And then, a long while passed in which I can't say what happened, except that the world seemed to darken to an unworldly degree. There were no more thoughts, at least none that I remember, though my senses were acute. The air with its coming dampness was a cool, delicate wetness on my face; I smelled its water-slogged leaves, heard its descent into the foliage as it quieted the winds rustling there. Maybe

I fell asleep then—I can't be sure—with the image of black bark, black bear imprinted on my eyelids. The next thing I remember is a sensation of riding a slow, water-bound roller coaster, inside my body, and then the pain of a nasty snap of the neck when I abruptly became conscious of my surroundings.

I was moving, there was no doubt. I wondered if this twilight awareness was fragile, if it would break apart with a sudden twitch, a loud noise. *Careful*, I thought, as if I were dreaming and must continue doing so at all costs. I kept my mind and my eyes forward, on the forest.

A bramble tore at me. There was a tug, but no sting of pain. My heart pounded; branches and weeds were running past me faster than I'd ever experienced, even when I'd had two legs to run on. I was running! I could feel the tufted ground beneath my feet, then the smoothness of pine needles, then rocks. I experimented with speeding up, slowing down, to see if I could do it without my state of mind, a fragile egg, sliding off its platter, and it worked. There was chill and dampness, yet I was warm.

Just on top of a hill, I stopped to look down. A lake, with a watery spear of moon lancing across it, rested in a valley. I bounded down to it without a thought and lowered my head to drink.

Surely I knew, after seeing my own reflection, that the situation had left the realm of the familiar. I say knew, though what I experienced was more of a physical awareness. It was all about feeling and smelling, listening.

Instinct.

I was tempted, on reflection, to compare the feeling to that of a drug effect, though I'd had little experience with drugs, except for the prescription kind. I was not dreamy or drowsy. I was strong, clear, alive.

Time was different, too; it was a memory. There was only a night full of running, stopping only to eat, drink, and lift my snout toward the stars.

Gradually, I made my way down a road whose appearance was familiar. I was wary and stopped to sniff.

I heard a low growl, and two large eyes zoomed past. I slipped into the woods and followed the eyes. They blinked off after a second, in front of a small house. There was a glint of metal on a porch.

A *porch*, I thought. A wave of familiarity stung me. I turned to run away from it and ran headlong into a human being, who screamed, then stopped and threw itself on the ground and lay still. A long, white tail fell along its back. I gave it a swat and another until it turned over and tried to get up. I reared up on my hind legs and roared. It ran toward the porch. I could see I'd scratched it; there was blood.

The house, its porch, its human, each was like an image under water that was slowly lifting into view. I knew them, though at the time, I couldn't name them. This was a place I'd escaped. I didn't want to return. Above me there was the sound of wings flapping, a reassuring sound that accompanied me all the way back to the woods.

The next thing I knew, I was struggling to stand, yanking at my paws to free them.

"Allan," said a voice.

Confined.

"Allan."

Confined. I jerked my head.

Above me several shapes stood.

One twitched near me.

A *beak*?

I closed my eyes.

"Allan, it's me."

Mrs. Gingerlake. With my eyes closed, I knew the voice instantly.

"I don't have much time to explain. You'll need to listen as well as you can. The bad news is you're trapped. You were injured inside the animal, and when that happens, there is no way back. Something about the injury changes your ability to—well—"

She was speaking very slowly and precisely. I thought I was dreaming, and smiled.

"The good news is you're no longer an invalid. And you're safe here."

"Where?"

I opened my eyes. A foot away, leaning down toward me, was a crow. It opened its beak again and spoke in Rita's voice. An image. The accident. Was I still in the ditch, with the sound of something dripping under me, a beeping somewhere inside the crumpled vehicle I couldn't identify? Had I imagined my whole life since? No. The hospital. The house. The peonies.

My reflection in a lake. I lifted my head and looked in the direction of the voice.

"Are you telling me I'm a bear, Rita?"

The crow bobbed its head toward her chest a few times.

"I didn't think you'd succeed, for God's sake. Almost no one does."

"Mrs. Gingerlake, is your voice coming from a crow?"

So this was why mixing whiskey and narcotics was a bad idea. I laughed. I was getting a huge kick out of this. It was ridiculous.

And then I cried. Because I was conscious. Awake. And a zebra was trying to comfort me, its hoof dangling delicately above my shoulder, giving me tiny pats. I shook it off. It laughed.

"Do I eat those?" I asked Mrs. Gingerlake.

"No. Allan, this isn't the wild. It's a sort of reserve. Think of it as a retirement home for animals. All sorts of animals, performers, strays, some like you who got stuck. There are thousands of acres. Plenty of food. And no cage unless you really need one."

"They're like me? Formerly . . ."

No words. I had no words left.

"Not all, a few. You'll find them. You're lucky, Allan, some people who get into this . . . situation . . . spend their lives alone. Out there."

The zebra shivered.

"This is the better alternative. Trust me."

Thousands of acres.

I put my energy into rolling over and standing up. The crow backed away, then leapt to a branch above me, folding and unfolding its claws around the branch, moving half inch by half inch away from me.

"Listen, you might be better prepared for a complete change of body than most people would be, but it's still a shock and you're not used to it."

Folding, unfolding.

"Get your bearings, before you try to do anything. I mean it, Allan. Just for a few days."

She had a point. Take it slow. I could do that. Hell, I was an expert at taking it slow. And from the perspective of my recent life and possibilities, the current state was an improvement. I couldn't write or have a brandy (could I?), but I could run. I was no longer a broken toy in a box at the end of a dead-end road.

By nightfall, I was in the hills and still hadn't come across any boundaries. In the valley, evening was beginning. A few lights twinkled at the farm. *Home*, I thought. The little cluster of buildings looked more welcoming than any I could remember.

Nearby, a twig broke, and I looked up to see a deer pondering me. It glanced over the valley and back again, chewed a leaf.

"Hello," I said.

It nodded and bounded away.

BREATHLESS

When Wilson walked, all he could hear was the sound of his breath. His lungs were a quagmire. He could only imagine what they'd look like if, God forbid, doctors ever had to cut him open for something. The strained breathing slowed him down some, but what he lacked in speed he made up for in endurance. Once his heart got to pumping in the fresh morning air, why, he could walk forever.

"There you are," he said, spotting the first glint of copper in the tall grass a few feet from the railroad tracks. What a specimen it was, almost perfectly oval, with a ragged silver ribbon running entirely round its edge where the copper had rubbed off. A rare thing. He took a plastic baggie from the chest pocket of his overalls and dropped it in.

He'd laid out fifty pennies on the tracks the day before, carefully spacing them a foot apart along the center of the rail. It wasn't as much effort as planting flower bulbs in the fall, and the results were immediate. He'd become addicted to immediate gratification, he thought, just like everybody else. But Wilson didn't have a garden anymore, and a man's got to do something to keep his mind from missing things.

One day when there were enough, he'd lay them out on the big table in his apartment. He'd make things, like wind chimes, the pennies dangling in ropes from little wooden caps. Or birdhouses with little copper roofs.

The next penny deceived him, lying next to a rusty tin can, and the next trembled on a stone like a dragonfly, wet from a nighttime storm that had been full of thunder but only the gentlest of rain, and there it stayed, balancing itself with a drop at each end. He wiped it off with a tissue. Wilson loved them all. Each was different, just like flowers. But a locomotive yielded a crop a day, and Wilson didn't have to worry about too little rain or an early freeze. There would always be another train.

On a day like today, with the storm clouds breaking up just above the tree line and the sun falling out of the holes between them, he could believe that time was only something human beings imagined. Maybe there would be no nursing home for him. Maybe his descent would stop with a loss of hearing and the words in the newspaper getting fuzzier every day, no matter how strong his glasses. He wiped his nose on his handkerchief. *It's all in how you look at things*, he thought.

Wilson counted the take so far. He never got them all. Some went missing and wouldn't be found no matter how far he wandered. Some stuck to the wheels, he thought, and dropped off miles away in another town.

He saw the deer before he heard it, a big buck standing on the tracks, ten penny-lengths away, as noble as any he'd ever shot and for that he was suddenly sorry. Then again, he'd been young in those days, and that's what young men did.

Any minute now, the buck would start and run the way deer do, crashing into the woods like a gun had gone off behind them. Far away before hunting season started.

"Hey, don't you know I'm dangerous?"

He laughed at himself, as threatening as a tree stump, his days as a predator long gone. The buck seemed to know it, bending its head to the grass growing between the rails, looking straight at Wilson without so much as a muscle twitch.

Wilson lifted a hand slowly to adjust his hearing aid. He thought he heard the sound of rain dripping off the leaves, but that was impossible. It was only his brain remembering. Sometimes he heard a mourning dove but saw an owl, or a cardinal's song coming from the beak of a robin until his eyes figured out what he was looking at, and then the sound corrected itself and he knew he wasn't really hearing it at all.

"Go on," Wilson said, checking his watch. The train was due. He stood up and continued his collecting. Penny by penny Wilson approached, and still the deer made no move. *Mighty peculiar*, he thought.

The baggie was heavy with coins. He jingled them, clapped them between his hands like a tambourine. "Shoo! Shoo!" he shouted. He was sweating. "Shoo!" He picked up a rock and threw it. It bounced off the track and into the grass with a ping Wilson only imagined hearing.

He took his handkerchief out of his pocket and dabbed at his forehead. As far as he could see, ahead or behind, there was nothing, no one. He felt the oddest sensation, as though time had stopped. The woods and sky were frozen in a painting of a perfect summer day. He didn't want to move and flutter the canvas.

The sun shed its clouds, and Wilson was suddenly very hot. He knelt on one knee to catch his breath.

The buck sniffed the air.

"Shoo," he said, and wheezed. The animal cocked his head, still watching him, and Wilson relaxed a little, until the train shot out of the clump of trees at the bend, its whistle screaming a warning to them both.

Wilson heard it too, by God. As deaf as he was, he could still hear a train whistle. His mouth opened, and he could have sworn the deer's did, too. Neither of them moved.

"Go," Wilson said.

The train barreled toward them, shutting out the sun.

"Go!" he shouted, but the buck's smooth brown pelt cracked into pieces with barely a sound. A shower of pennies started above Wilson's head and glinted in the sunlight as they dropped to the earth, with tiny sounds he heard as summer hail.

JUNCTION, COUNTY T

The walk that led to his parents' house was lined with peonies, as it always was in the spring. This was his house too, though he'd grown out of living there, and now just at daybreak the sun lit up the clapboard in sharp relief. A glowing snapshot of his history, trembling in the morning air, dissolving.

Once he walked down that sidewalk there was no going back. He would hear his mother call out, and his father would ask her who is it, who is there, from his chair in front of the television where nothing had changed.

There were a lot of bad things Jack could have done. He could have gotten someone pregnant, been fired from his job. Anything would have been easier than what he was about to tell them.

Out of habit, he locked the car. He opened the trunk and pulled out his gym bag, into which he'd thrown a toothbrush, a change of clothes, and, at the last minute, the passport he'd gotten for spring break his last year in college.

He could hear the rattle of canned applause through the open window. There was a ratty screen door that didn't quite close, the smell of coffee just made. A carton of milk sat on the counter next to the sink.

"Well!" His mother wiped her hands on a towel. "What got you up so early?"

"Evelyn, is that Jack?"

Jack tried to breathe deeply, as he had at his apartment. He'd put laundry in the basket he kept in the bedroom, thrown the perishables out of the fridge, been in constant motion as if it could keep his mind from overtaking him. He'd beaten down the images, until now. Seeing his parents made him feel safe, and safety made him feel weak. He started to cry.

"Jack?" His mother looked frightened. "Lloyd! Come out here," she shouted.

Jack took a breath.

His father came into the room, looked at the two of them, his grown son crying, his wife's ashen face. He moved to comfort her, and they waited for Jack to speak.

There was a noise outside. Jack looked out. He couldn't see anyone, but the neighborhood was full of elderly people, as likely to weed the garden at the crack of dawn as at two in the afternoon.

"Close the window," he said.

"What?"

"Close the window, Ma."

Over the sink, the window was open. She pulled it down. A small jar filled with colored marbles and glitter sat on the sill. He'd made it in first grade.

There were no new words for it, so he used old ones. "I'm sorry," he said. "I'm sorry!"

"For crying out loud, Jack," said his father. "Straighten up, come on. Nothing's that bad."

Jack closed his eyes, tried to straighten up. "This is that bad," he said, hoping his dad was right and knowing he wasn't. "I'm in trouble."

His mother instinctively closed the front door, glancing out the window first. They were not the kind of family that liked to make a show.

"Have you got a drink?" Jack asked.

"It's six thirty in the morning!" His father hesitated, but after another look at Jack's face went to the refrigerator and brought out a beer. "We got nothing stronger."

"Let's sit down," Jack said. His father pulled out a chair for his mother.

Jack hesitated.

"Well for Christ's sake," said his father.

"But you look all right," said his mother, looking for a black eye or broken arm.

Jack spoke slowly. It would be better if he only had to say it once.

He'd had an accident, he said, and laughed. Nerves. His stomach turned with a thump.

There was a dent in the front of his car, a big one that changed the face of his Toyota, its calm mouth now a grimace. And if that dent had held the shape of a deer or some other wild animal stupid enough to cross his path, all would still have been well.

It was possible there was blood in the grill, where the bulk of a man's body had slammed and fell, maybe blood on the tires. His mother clapped her hand over her mouth.

He'd been drunk and had kept on driving, trying to pretend he was too drunk to know what he'd done. Eventually, panic broke through the fog. He turned around.

The man was on his back, unmoving, unblinking, undeniably dead. Jack had a moment of complete sobriety, long enough to wonder what the hell the guy had been doing walking down a country road at what, midnight? One in the morning? The middle of nowhere. And then Jack got scared, primitively scared, and jumped in his car and drove away. He couldn't think what else to do.

For a while his parents said nothing. His father cried as fathers do, eyes filling up and then a Herculean effort to stop them. He ran his hand over the top of his head.

As he's always done, thought Jack, and it was beautiful and he loved him for it.

The confession was over.

His mother got a beer for his father and even for herself, something Jack had only seen her do twice, though he couldn't remember why.

"We have to call the police," she said, holding the beer while his father opened it and tossed the cap onto the counter. She sipped and made a face, then sipped again.

Jack's father studied the butter dish on the kitchen table.

"Did anyone see you?" he asked.

"Lloyd! What difference does that make? You can't be thinking— we need to call the police!" His mother tried again to sip her beer.

No one had seen him. Country roads in the rural Midwest didn't have cameras, and cops were as rare as banks. But Jack watched plenty of television. People don't get away with murder anymore. He could barely think of the word without wanting to pass out. Sooner or later . . . but he was guilty. It didn't matter that he hadn't been seen. Or did it?

He'd come to his parents for the strength to confess, he said.

His father shook his head. "Where's the car?"

"In the driveway."

Lloyd looked startled and pushed his chair back with a scrape. He put a hand out to stop his wife from following. "No, Evelyn. We don't all three have to be out there. You too," he told Jack. "Stay here."

His mother came to him, bent down, and hugged him. Her hair was scratchy and smelled like hair spray. She'd had a permanent. Tomorrow was Sunday. Church.

His father took a set of keys off the key holder next to the stove.

"Give me your keys, Jack."

"What? Why?"

"Give me your keys."

Jack stood up and got his keys out of his jeans pocket and handed them to him.

"What are you doing?"

Lloyd didn't answer.

Jack and his mother watched from the door as his father backed Jack's car out of the driveway and parked it on the street, and then backed his own car out of the garage and parked it on the other side. He got back in the Toyota and pulled it into the garage as fast as Jack had ever seen him drive, and then calmly pulled his old Plymouth into the driveway. He shut the garage door and walked back in.

"We have to talk about this."

Jack felt sick. He'd seen his father like this before and recognized the boundless, protective energy that had saved Jack when he'd been suspended in high school for skipping class, or when he was kicked off the football team for smoking pot, or when he'd been evicted from his first apartment because of a loud party. Lloyd didn't have money, but he was resourceful. He knew how to talk to people. Jack learned to stand off to the side, looking humble and sorry, while his father worked out the problem, promised that his son had learned his lesson. No problem is too big, Jack, if you set your mind to it, he'd said. Lloyd had never been one to cut his losses and quit.

"This isn't something you can fix!" His mother began to cry.

"Let's just think about this calmly. Not fly off the handle, let's just think about it." Lloyd turned back to his son. "Jack, do you realize the trouble you're in? Do you realize—"

"But we can't fix it."

"You give up too easy, Jack. You always have, and you can't this time. For once in your life, listen to me. We can solve this thing."

Evelyn set the beer can down with a hollow plink, her cheeks red.

"What on earth are you thinking? What can you possibly do? We've got to call the police. He's killed a man!"

"Calm down. Calm down, come on now." His father put his arm around her. Jack hadn't seen him do that in years. They'd been getting along, Jack realized. Better these last few years with Jack out of the house.

Lloyd pulled a chair out and guided her into it. He handed her a napkin. "Here." She wiped at her cheeks.

"Now tell us again. Start from the beginning."

The phone rang. Lloyd made a beeline for it. Jack's heart pounded in his chest.

"Yello," his father said into the receiver. Jack laughed, and so did his mother, because they couldn't help it.

"Just about the Legion meeting tonight," his father said, and came back to the table.

"This early? Who would call at this time of the—"

Lloyd waved a hand at her and turned his attention back to Jack.

"Okay, start over. What time did you leave the bar? Who were you with?"

Jack told them the whole story again.

He remembered everything, except for the exact moment of impact, of that he was positive. There had been no blackout. In fact, he was pretty sure he'd only had four, maybe five drinks all evening, a shot or two someone bought. He was also sure that when he left his coworkers, they would have thought he was in better shape than they were. His father nodded.

"Did you hear anything on the news this morning? Surely if there was a man laying in the middle of County T, it would be on the news! Someone has to have come upon it by now." His mother's voice rose.

"Time to go see," said Lloyd. They followed him into the living room. A recording of last week's baseball flashed off as Lloyd clicked to a news station and put the volume up.

"Get me another beer." He winked to apologize for the abrupt tone his wife didn't seem to notice anyway.

A car commercial came on.

"You're going to have to pull yourself together before you go back to work," his father said.

"I'm off," said Jack. "I'm off next week. That's why I went out for a drink. Vacation." He shrugged. "I was going to paint my apartment."

"You'd better stay here, at least for the weekend, until we can get this sorted out. You're sure no one drove by while you were stopped or—"

"Yeah, I'm sure. I was upset, but still, if there had been someone, they would have stopped, don't you think?"

"Not necessarily, not in the middle of the night. What if it was a woman out there, driving home alone? She might drive by. Though, if she'd seen what you claim was there, she would have called someone."

"No one went by. It was late. Besides, there's hardly any traffic on that road, even in the daytime."

"And then you went home?"

"That's the part I'm blurry on. I mean, I know I didn't stop anywhere, but the actual trip home is kind of—"

"What did you do when you got there?"

"A lot of things, I don't know. Why?"

"You didn't call anyone, did you?"

"No. And I didn't go to bed because I was sure the cops were going to come. And then when nothing happened, I got up the nerve to leave and come here."

"Have you eaten?" his mother asked.

He shook his head.

"I'll make some toast. Come on. You can see the television from the kitchen."

His father leaned forward in his chair in the living room, fingers adjusting his hearing aid as he watched the screen. Every few seconds, he flipped to another local news channel. They all had the same stories: a house burned down on Fifth Street, a fundraiser scheduled for the family that had lived there, the robbery of a gas station by a local teenager desperate for a cigarette and a Coke.

His father turned around in his easy chair and looked at him. "Tell me exactly where you were. *If* you know."

Jack put down his toast. "I remember seeing that red barn on County T, the one with the big searchlights."

"Show me."

"What?"

"Eat. Then we're going for a drive."

"Do you think that's wise? Won't they be watching for the criminal to return to the scene of the crime?" His mother had a point.

"So what if they are? We're a family on our way to breakfast. What's that place over in Hedge Lake?"

"The Bun Basket," said his mother.

"Then that's where we're headed, if anyone asks. Obviously, we'll take our car."

She handed Jack a few pieces of bacon, and he ate. No matter what had happened, he could always count on his appetite.

"It's going to be okay," his dad said as the three of them walked out to the car, trying to act normal.

Jack hoped the neighbors wouldn't come out. The three of them looked like hell. His mother's eyes were bloodshot and red-rimmed like his own. His father's hands shook as he put the key in the passenger door and helped his wife into the car.

"As usual," he said as Ed and Shelly Lambert came out onto the porch next door with their coffee mugs. "Wave at them, Evelyn."

His mother smiled and waved. "We'll take our time. Hopefully they'll have gone in by the time we get back."

The lights inside Gustaf's market were just coming on. Jack had run there for his mother a million times. He knew the aisles by heart: deodorants and hair dyes, sunglasses, the photo counter where he'd collected thick packets full of awkward pictures of family picnics and birthday parties. Jack felt his eyes well up.

Straighten up, he told himself, but the dread was overwhelming. It was alien, out of his control, no matter how many deep breaths he took. No matter how many beers he had, he'd never be drunk enough to forget this.

Lloyd's eyes focused on the traffic straight ahead. His face was calm, but sweat beaded on the sides of his forehead, his wispy hair stuck to his head.

Gradually, the houses thinned out and the road was framed by farm fields.

"Get my sunglasses out of there, would you? Harder to see in this light than in the damn dark."

His mother opened the glove compartment and got his father's sunglasses out of a faded leather pouch. "Want a peppermint?"

His father put out a hand out of habit, and so did Jack.

The whole scene threatened to break him.

His parents had waited longer than most for a child, adopting when the usual method didn't work, and, though Jack wasn't quite twenty-five, Lloyd was already over seventy, still trying to make up for being too old to do the things that other fathers did with their sons. Still cleaning up after him, all because Jack had had too much to drink at a bar with his coworkers, people he didn't even especially like. He'd been bored. Waiting for a polite way out from the minute he got there. Yet he'd stayed just a little too long. Eventually the alcohol convinced him he was having a swell time. What he'd give to have that boredom back, to be sitting on a barstool tuning out the small talk, grinning stupidly over the noise of the jukebox.

But this day he wanted to go on forever, just the three of them, a team, trying to make the best of things. The weather was warm and breezy. It was a perfect day to help his dad around the yard.

It was also a nightmare. But Jack was awake, alive, aware of everything in a way he hadn't been in years, maybe ever.

"Where is that place again? Twenty, thirty miles out?"

"It's past the cottages," Jack said.

"Oh, the cobblestone cottages in front of Pelican Lake!" said his mother. "You remember those, Jack?"

There were ten of them. They looked like fairy houses with their whimsical peaked roofs and wildflower gardens. When he was little, the cottages were sort of an attraction. Families drove out to see them on Sundays after church. There had been no casinos then, or video games, or texting.

"And then comes the lake," said his father.

"And then the curve in the road where that house is with the little white bridge in the front yard where the creek goes through, the big field with the birches right in the middle of it—" said his mother.

"And then the red barn," Jack finished, and they were quiet again.

They passed the first of the cobblestone cottages, and then there was the water itself, just visible through a broad gap in the trees. Gradually, the trees closed up again, and the road curved.

Lloyd slowed as they passed a sign that said "Junction, County T."

"Okay," he said. "This should be it."

"Can I get in the front? I can't see well enough back here," said Jack.

"Gingerly, gingerly." Lloyd checked the rearview mirror and stopped the car.

Jack changed places with his mother and studied the road in front of them.

The bar Jack had been drinking in was only a mile further up the road. The roadsides held no answers. Nothing but gutters full of crabgrass, the occasional can or snack wrapper. And beyond those, barbed wire fencing to keep the local livestock from wandering down County T.

"There are the birches. Was it before or after the birches?" his mother asked.

"I don't know. I remember the birches, because they're so white in the dark. I remember that."

"But you were going the wrong way to see the birches. Unless this is where you turned around, which would mean . . ."

They all got quiet for a minute.

"The body should be here. After it happened, I drove off, and then I turned around and went back—"

"We're going to Animal's," Jack's father said. He stepped on the gas.

They approached the bar slowly. It would open in a few hours for the Sunday afternoon softball crowd, but, for now, it was dark. Jack looked away. He never wanted to see the place again. The irony, he thought, was that he probably never would.

"I didn't hit him here, Dad."

His father again checked the mirrors and did a U-turn in the road.

"That's all there is, Jack. We must have passed it. How long did you drive after you hit him until you realized you had to go back?"

"God, I don't know! I don't know. Thirty seconds? Half an hour? I don't know."

"It couldn't have been half an hour, Jack; we were in town half an hour ago. I'm guessing it was more like a minute. Nobody's got a sense of time when they're loaded. That's why people shouldn't be driving cars in that condition."

Jack was acutely aware that his father had been drinking before getting in the car this morning, although as he said and Jack felt, they could only hope to feel it. For now, adrenaline was keeping the fog at bay.

"The road was straight, I know it was," Jack said, but he doubted himself.

They went as slowly as they thought they could without looking suspicious, up and down the same few miles of road a half-dozen times, but there was nothing, just clear blacktop. No skid marks, no dark stains, no sign of anything being other than it should be.

His dad turned the car around for one last time and headed back toward town.

Jack wished he would wake up with a hangover and the residue of a crazy dream to shake off in the shower. He was exhausted, and, from the looks of his parents, so were they. They drove home quietly, his father almost running a stop sign on the way.

"This is awful," said his mother.

"I know, Mom. I'm sorry." Jack started to cry again.

It was only 10:00 a.m., and she stood staring at the muted TV set, rubbing her hands on her blouse as if she were still wearing her breakfast apron. "Go upstairs for a while, Jack. Get some sleep," she said. "You look terrible."

He climbed the stairs to his childhood bedroom and closed the door behind him. *Safe.*

The radio on the nightstand was broken now. It was just like his parents not to throw it away but leave it there because someday they'd fix it. The dresser no longer held his clothes but extra sheets, half-spent candles, miscellaneous things that had nowhere else to go. Not everything revolved around him anymore. That was a good thing, he supposed. He nosed around in the closet, wiped a layer of dust from a box marked "Holiday Decorations." Inside were his mother's pickle ornaments, his favorites. They'd always been fragile, but now there were widening spots of silver where the delicate green paint had flaked off. He rewrapped them and gently set them back in the box.

He hadn't yet reached the age when memories become magical and precious, important to remember. He carried them carelessly, because they were still so close behind. Now, they crowded him, gently at first, softly like the blanket on his childhood bed. But the enormity of what he'd done, what he was about to lose, gave them louder voices, all clamoring for a place in his mind. Crickets outside his bedroom window at the edge of the woods, the Halloween costumes his mother had sewn from his father's old work clothes, crusty snowbanks at the edge of the field across the road. His life clutched at his heart and tried to wake him.

But he was in his parents' house. Surely, no darkness could find its way through the leaves of the maple tree outside the window and into this room.

For a few hours, he would leave it alone, for their sake. And then he would call the police. He got down on his knees and prayed that if anyone was listening, thank you for his life, and for the last morning he'd had with his parents, and please make the rest of their lives a cakewalk. He slept like the dead until his mother called to him from the landing.

"Jack! It's getting late. Jack? Supper."

He lifted himself up and pulled his pants from the rumpled pile next to the bed. For a second he didn't remember what he was doing there. Then dread moved him slowly, as if the carpet were trying to close itself around his feet.

Suppertime. A squirrel eating the birdseed from the feeder outside the kitchen window, his mother's hands working in the sink in the timeless light of late afternoon.

"Nothing. There's not a damn thing on the news about it," his father said. "If you were high on pot, tell us now, Jack. I don't need this. We don't need this."

"Are you kidding? Do you think I imagined it because I was smoking pot? Believe me, if I had been, none of this would have happened."

"What wouldn't have happened? Looks like nothing did, Jack, except you had some kind of accident, that's plain to see."

Jack was flabbergasted. The road trip had given his father hope. He was annoyed, as if all Jack had done was put a dent in his father's car on the way home from school. Jack's stomach lurched.

He sat down at the table and looked at a plate of white bread, lunch meat, and a jar of pickles. Not his mother's usual meal.

"Evelyn, I'm going to get dressed." His father left the room and Jack heard his footsteps on the stairs.

"Dad's not eating?"

"He already ate. It's late."

Jack glanced at the clock. It was past five. His parents had eaten supper at four, without fail, ever since Lloyd had retired.

"Jack, I don't know what to think," his mother said. "You understand that, don't you? Your dad doesn't know what to think either. He wants to help you, but what can he do?"

"Would he have been happier if we'd found a body? Would that have made everything okay?"

"But where is it? Is it possible you just hit something else?" Her face fell. "My God, Jack, what if you did hit a man, and he crawled off somewhere, just out of sight?"

He shook his head. "Ma, I have to call the police."

She glanced at the stairs and lowered her voice. "Calm down."

"We should talk to Dad. It'll be worse if I wait."

She lowered her voice. "He's not going to want to talk to you for a while."

No, he wouldn't. Jack had let him down. Lloyd had no tolerance for gray areas, secretive shenanigans. Something that wasn't what it seemed had driven him crazy when Jack was a boy: the musty odor of pot he couldn't put his finger on, the teenage son late getting home and the details unclear. And Lloyd's face disappointed and clouded with worry like any parent, but also angry that he couldn't solve the problem. He'd looked the same way that morning, scanning the county road for answers and finding none.

It occurred to Jack that if he had come home with a body in his trunk, Lloyd would have known what to do. He imagined his father in the moonlight out in Matelski's field, wearing his gray coveralls, handing Jack a shovel. It didn't seem that far-fetched.

"Lloyd! You're going to be late."

"Evelyn, where are my reading glasses?" Lloyd hurried down the stairs while Jack's mother bustled around the living room, gathering the reading glasses, the minutes from the last Legion meeting, Lloyd's wallet.

From the window, he watched his father walk down the sidewalk in a short-sleeved shirt and tie, pointy Legion cap perched on his head. Concentrating.

Giving his father a problem he couldn't solve was unfair at this stage of the game, the worst thing Jack could have done.

The light was on in the living room. His mother sat in the chair on the right side of the lamp, her finger in the loop of a coffee mug. His father's empty chair was on the left side of it, the TV soundless against the opposite wall.

He got a beer and one for his mother. He figured if she didn't want one he'd drink two. She took it.

"It will help me sleep," she said. "Do you want something to eat?"

He shook his head.

"No. Dad get home?"

"He went up to bed about an hour ago. Mad about the Legion meeting." She smiled.

"What was it this time?"

"Oh, Roy again. He was supposed to get the flags down from the posts after the Memorial Day doings and bring them back tonight. He didn't do either. They're expensive, those flags." She clicked through the channels. "It's his own fault. He knows better than to trust Roy. You know he still drinks like a fish."

"Yeah," said Jack. Roy had gone to war with Lloyd, and war buddies were sacred no matter what they'd become once they returned home. Not all of them had fared well, not even after years of normal life. His father watched over them like he'd watched over Jack. And now they were thinning out.

"You mark my words: he'll get up tomorrow and go get them himself."

Jack doubted that. There were bigger problems. He sat looking at the faces of young women with healthy, flowing hair as a bottle of shampoo floated across the screen on a rainbow of jewels.

In the morning, his father wouldn't look at him and pushed his eggs around his plate with a piece of toast. From where he stood, Jack had taken them on a wild goose chase and there was nothing to show for it.

His mother lifted a few pieces of bacon from a plate in the center of the table, careful not to meet Jack's eyes. At the end of what seemed like ten minutes, Lloyd threw his toast down. It made a scratchy sound on the plate.

"What are you going to do about the car? Have you thought about that?"

His words implied there was no longer a "we." It was Jack's problem. *Fair enough*, Jack thought. "I don't know."

"I suggest you think about it." Lloyd got up and went into the living room.

"You know your dad's right about the car."

"But what do you think, Mom? I can just take it to the mechanic and get it fixed? Anywhere I go for miles, they'll be looking for it."

The front door slammed.

"Where on earth is he going now?" His mother stood and looked out the window in the door. "He's in the garage."

"I'll go see," said Jack. He went to the garage.

"Shut the door," said Lloyd. He was digging through an old red metal toolbox. He chose a screwdriver and knelt next to the license plate.

Jack laughed in spite of himself.

Lloyd glared at him. He removed the license plate on the back of the car, then the front, tossing them both with a clank onto the floor. He stood up and tried to open the driver's side door.

"What's going on?" his mother asked.

Jack shrugged.

His father was stuffing the license plates into a garbage bag along with the contents of the Shop Vac he kept in the garage.

"Get me a file."

Lloyd flung open the driver's side door and took his glasses out of his pocket. He began to file away the vehicle identification number from the inside of the frame, and Jack watched, feeling helpless, just as he had as a child. He was the assistant, aiming a flashlight into a car engine or holding a piece of lumber at one end while his dad ran it through the table saw. *Don't pull on it. Just hold it so it doesn't drop when the saw goes through.* Jack had tried hard to do things right. And Lloyd took care of him, protected him as though he was breakable. It had to end, should have ended long ago.

"I should be calling the police."

His father put the file down and leaned on the tool counter with both hands. Jack could see him trembling.

"We can't hide a whole car," Jack said.

"It will ruin everything. Your life will be over."

"My life is already over."

"Stop it! You had an *accident*." He lowered his voice and drew closer. "Maybe, just maybe, you killed someone, Jack. Could have been one of those drug addicts from the halfway house out there. But we don't know for sure. Look, if this were something small, I'd say go ahead, tell the police, but this is prison, Jack. Think about what that would do to your mother." His voice cracked.

Jack leaned against the car.

His father dug through his tools. He got out a couple of screwdrivers and handed one to Jack. He opened the driver's side door and sat on the seat, removed the rearview mirror, and tossed it out.

"Get me the wire cutter. And take off that other mirror."

Jack did as he was told.

His father cut the wires to the steering column and tossed it out.

"Get some of those crates, over there, the ones stacked up in the corner. We can put some of this stuff in them."

By noon, the seats were taken out and sawed in half; the CD player lay on the tool cabinet; the mirrors, dashboard, and doors were off; and the battery sat on a towel.

"But these are little things! The rest . . . how can we possibly take that apart? It's too big! It can't be done," Jack said.

"Put these crates in my trunk. We're making a run to the dump."

"Don't they have a watchman? He'll see us."

"Then we tell him we cleaned out the garage. I'm a resident of this county, and, by God, I've got a permit to use the dump."

Jack and his father made the trip in silence. At the edge of the dump was a sentry box of sorts, and from the inside came a man with a cap on, wiping his hands on a rag. Jack's father held the permit up for him to see.

"Whatcha got, buddy?"

"Just cleaned out the garage."

"No chemicals, batteries, or explosives?"

"Nope."

He waved them in.

"I'll pop the trunk, you toss the stuff."

They drove to a bin marked "Metals," and Jack emptied the bent front grill, the mirrors, and then on to "Plastics" where they dumped the steering column and the dashboard contents, then "Other" where they dumped the seats.

"Then, of course, we've got the tires. Are they any good? I hate to throw away good tires."

"They won't fit on your car, Dad. You'd have to give them to someone, and how would you explain where you got those?"

"For now, they'll go up in the storage loft with the rest of the nonsense that's up there. Anyone wants to dig through all that, I'd be surprised."

Jack looked at his mother, who seemed unfazed. Tolerance, he thought. She was letting Lloyd process things the way he needed to, confident that at some point he'd arrive at the obvious.

His mother fixed them grilled cheese sandwiches, busying and fussing as though they'd been outside cleaning the windows. After lunch, Jack and his father went back to the garage.

The car was a shell. But it was still a car. Inside the house, the phone rang. They both looked up, but the minutes passed, and the two went back to work.

"Damn," said his father, walking around and around. "Damn." He waved a hand. "It can be done. You know, Jack, the whole thing could end up no bigger than a Rubik's Cube, if we want." His voice trailed off.

"I've got an idea." He put a finger in the air and waggled it. "One little idea, Jack, that's all it takes. You'll see. I've got a blowtorch. But that's only part of it."

Jack smiled in spite of himself. Lloyd held the torch to the car, and they watched the paint turn orange in the flame, melting inward like taffy.

"Just look at her go! What did I tell you? Rubik's Cube, Jack."

The door opened. His mother stood there, in her green slacks and flowered blouse, pale and staring at both of them.

"Stop it," she said.

"What?" Jack asked.

"Stop."

Lloyd lifted his hands up. "What?"

"Roy's dead."

"What?" Lloyd asked.

"That's why he didn't take the flags down." She put a hand on her chest. "Jack."

Jack froze.

His mother just stood there, shaking her head. "He was walking home. On County T."

Lloyd gasped.

"But I would have—" Jack started but then realized he hadn't seen Roy Messer in years. The face he'd seen that night could have belonged to anyone.

"It can't be! Nobody called us, it wasn't on the news—"

"They kept it quiet until Helen could get ahold of the kids."

"But there were no cops out there, nothing. I don't understand," said Jack.

Lloyd brought his hands down on the workbench and lurched forward over it.

Jack tried to move toward him, comfort him. But his father's shrunken demeanor told him to stay back. He'd never seen him like that, not ever. Unmoving, stiff.

Minutes passed.

Lloyd began to brush the dust from the surface of the workbench.

"God knows he wasn't much of a man, but he didn't deserve this, didn't deserve to be mown down like—"

"No one would have deserved it," said his mother.

"No. No," Lloyd said. His eyes were brimming, full of bewilderment and betrayal. He wiped them on a rag streaked with grease and walked into the house.

"I'm sorry, I have to—" His mother looked toward the kitchen.

"It's okay," Jack said.

She closed the door, leaving him to stare after her, helpless in the rubble of his crime.

It was over, wasn't it? He knew what to do, yet he couldn't. Until something occurred to him. An image. A memory. Himself, a child, alone at the kitchen table amid a pile of books and papers, cheeks tear-stained. But *working*. Thankful to his father for filling the space where his own will should have been.

He closed his eyes. *Do not leave this table until you've finished your work.*

This time, he would finish. He would do what his father had always wanted him to do, whether he realized it or not.

Jack pulled out his phone and dialed.

SAVIOR

Her name was Ann Gardner, and Ray was not afraid of her.

He lifted his head to see what she was doing outside the car. So much effort. He imagined the veins standing out on his neck, purple under his papery skin.

She'd made him comfortable, as much as was possible for a tall man squeezed into a short space. Soft pillows held him in a half-sitting position in the back seat, his shoulders against the passenger door. Two thin blankets tucked in at his sides. She'd even wedged a cardboard box behind the driver's seat, bottom side up, so he could stretch a leg a little and rest his foot on it.

The first day he'd met her, Ray heard only her voice. Bits of conversation from the kitchen, first his daughter Patsy's usual drone, then a new voice, a stranger, who would have to suffer through Patsy's chatter like everyone else. He could make out snatches, enough to recognize a familiar fabrication about the house's history, this one about a dead novelist and a ghost with a tale to tell. Pure fiction.

But it was October. Halloween was around the corner, this much he knew. So the tale, always long, would certainly grow. And here was a reporter from the local paper who'd drawn the short straw.

Footsteps in the hall. Closer as Patsy unpacked in shrill voice the romance that had ended when one of the novelist's lovers hanged himself in the foyer. The kids giggling.

Patsy and the reporter paused briefly at the door to the living room. He lay on the couch, its old cushions sinking in the middle, threatening to swallow him whole. And then he heard his name mentioned, as if something not to be minded.

The new voice, almost a whisper, but plain enough to hear. "My father died last month," the woman said.

"Oh," said Patsy, "too bad," and clomped on to the next scene of the supernatural.

From his position, only the tops of the trees were visible. Poplar leaves shimmered above thin branches as one body until the wind shattered them into hundreds of tiny whirling pieces.

Ann was outside the car, leaning against the door, one hand in her pocket, the other holding a cigarette. She smoked, wiped at her cheeks.

She was upset about him.

"It's not that bad," Ray said, but Ann couldn't hear him.

She got back into the car, bringing with her the sound of waves from outside. Waves! How long had it been since he'd heard that sound? Waves pushing each other onto the beach, overlapping, shrinking back into the lake, pushing out again. It was a sure thing. It could be counted on. It breathed.

She settled into the seat and turned to face him. "We're close to the water, Ray," she said.

Cool air lingered about the half-open window behind his head. He wanted to be cold, to feel anything still left to be felt at this late hour of his life. A raindrop found its way to the top of his head and inched along his cheekbone. A few more might wash away the grime of age and illness. Enough of them might be a miracle.

Sometimes, when he opened his eyes in the blackness, he feared she'd gone. His eyes were poor and struggled to adjust, watching as her face gradually became clearer, her hair messy and loose over her collar. He needn't have worried. Every time he woke, she was awake. Every time he whispered, she responded.

Now he lifted his arm. It made the smallest rustle, one the din of sunshine would have drowned out, but the darkness let through.

A match lit her face and reflected off the glass behind her. "Hey," she said.

He cleared his throat.

"Ray? Are you okay? Do you need anything?" She lifted the bag of morphine syringes. The liquid inside glowed like copper before she shook the match with a curse. It was shocking the way women swore these days. She lit another.

He shook his head. Ray felt no pain and was surprised. Ann was right: his family had been giving him too much. Without it, death was a strange and simple thing. His thoughts hung in a haze above his body, unable to make an impact, as if his feelings were detaching themselves one by one. It was not that simple for Ann. Both her feet were still planted in the world. He tried to keep hold of that thought, so he could help.

"It's after midnight," she said. "The clouds are blowing off, Ray. I think it's going to be a clear night after all."

He imagined the moon filling in the cracks between the clouds.

She unscrewed the cap of her flask and took a sip, then drew some brandy into the dropper and released it into his mouth. It was bitter and warm. He closed his eyes to savor it.

Patsy and the kids had gone outside so that Ann could "get the feel of things."

She sat with a plunk in the chair in the foyer.

He could just see her silhouette.

"Ghosts my ass," she said, taking a small notebook out of her coat pocket. She grumbled, looked around, shrugged off her coat, and tiptoed around the room as one does in the house of someone else. She was curious. Ray wanted to tell her she wasn't likely to find ghosts in the cupboards.

And then she found him. She stopped short at the entrance to the living room and sucked in her breath. He was feeling livelier then, awake enough to infuse sound into a greeting.

"Hello," he said.

She felt for the opening of the pocket and pushed the notebook back in. "Do you think there's a ghost here?" she asked.

"No," he said, "just me."

She laughed. "You're the ghost."

He laughed too, a small wheeze that made his head fall off the pillow. She came over and lifted it up, crunching the fabric beneath his neck so he wouldn't have to try so hard to keep it in place. "Who are you?" he asked.

"I'm a reporter for the *Mercy Lake Times*. Human interest stuff. Your daughter called about a haunted house, so here I am."

"Too bad for you," he said.

He fell asleep, the kind of sleep he'd been having now, deep sleep punctuated by wakefulness. At times, the two states were indistinguishable from one another, and, truthfully, that first time he woke, he didn't remember she'd been there until she returned, the next day and the next. He looked forward to her visits and forgot to think them out of place.

"Shit, there's a car coming." She slid down in the driver's seat and twisted toward him, keeping her head low, and reached a hand between the seats.

"Sorry, Ray," she said, "it's only for a minute." She pulled the blanket over his head. He tried to make himself small, but there was nowhere for him to go. The blanket smelled like laundry soap and itched his nose. If he wiggled his eyebrows, he could move it or puff it out around his mouth with a breath.

"Don't make any sudden moves," she joked.

A light passed over the inside of the car, outlining her worried face pressed against the center console, coat shoved up around her chin. It went out.

"They're gone." She pulled the blanket away from his face and closed his hands around it. "No worries."

Ray wasn't worried. He felt like a fugitive, which, at this stage of the game, was a pleasant and humorous surprise.

She turned on the engine to warm him. There was music, some kind of jazz. Then a piano, with static in between as she turned the knob.

"My dad liked the most awful music," she said.

She told him she'd gotten a call, no time for goodbyes. She'd cleaned out her father's apartment. Young women were always making heroes of their fathers. That was all right, Ray thought. And the fact that he was probably a stand-in was all right, too. He hadn't been a hero to Patsy, but he had been a soldier, and a good husband. Life had been years and years of ordinary days until his wife's death and his own illness made every day seem unreal and groundless.

Patsy, whom he was beginning to suspect he'd failed in some alarming way, had moved into his house with her kids and her discontent. She complained to everyone who would listen that she had to take care of Ray. But she wasn't up to the task. Almost from the start, taking care of him seemed to annoy her. She preferred to tend to the house. Patsy had only been punctuation in his long life. But that was the way with fathers and daughters then.

So she painted and rearranged and pulled boxes out of corners and hauled them down from the attic. The kids played with them on their way to the garbage bins outside.

How far away it all seemed. His house, the voices of his family.

His introspection was interrupted by the radio. He and Ann heard the bulletin as clearly as if the announcer were in the car with them. Ray's name. Ann's name. A description of the car.

"Oh my god," she said. She pushed her hair out of her face, took out a cigarette, and, glancing at Ray, put it away.

Ann was not believed to be dangerous, the voice said. His daughter wanted him to stay calm. She would find him.

"Jesus Christ." Ann took a drink.

"I'm happy," he said. *For the first time in so long*, he thought.

Ann would never be certain of that. If he'd been stronger, he would have told her. And he'd have told Patsy that he had been paying attention. He remembered the kind little girl who let her mother win at cards. Life had given Patsy a beating. She was doing the best she could.

So many thoughts occurring. He had to let them go, because the only task ahead of him was at hand. Already!

Ray didn't blame Ann for what she'd done. He could see how things must have looked, the squalor in the house and Patsy so sharp and bitter. The family did their own living elsewhere in the house so as not to disturb him. That's what they said, but he knew it wasn't true. Nobody wants to watch an old man die.

But they kept up with the morphine, amber drops falling into his mouth, tingly and bitter as it soaked into the tender skin inside his cheek. Always it moved him, inside, as physically as if he were a tractor downshifted on a hill. His family argued and fussed, made him feel he had to keep still and hurry up at the same time. It took energy he didn't have. His strength was leaking out of him, and no replacement was coming.

Ann pulled a wooden chair from the kitchen and set it next to the couch. He tipped his head up dutifully for water. She talked while she straightened his sheets, picked up his blanket and gave it a snap, replaced it, sat down again. The blanket left a cloud of dust that settled and blended into the grime already thick on the arms of chairs and the tops of tables in the room.

"Ray? Have you been in pain?" She examined the morphine droppers on the stand next to the bed.

He shook his head.

"Three less than yesterday," she said.

He nodded.

The door opened. Ann backed her chair up a bit. Patsy looked at the two of them, a cigarette twitching impatiently between her lips.

"Well, you two are certainly getting chummy."

"I thought he might have seen something."

Patsy laughed. "It's the rest of the house that's haunted. That's where the action is. The attic. The basement."

Ann was pretty sure she'd find a skeleton or spooky scene rigged up in one of those places for her benefit.

"Listen, as long as you're interviewing him"—she snorted—"maybe you could stay for a couple hours so I can take the kids to a movie. They haven't been out in weeks, except to school."

"Well, I don't know. I mean I really should get back to the paper."

Patsy had already put on a jacket. Car keys dangled in her hand. She waited.

Ann looked at Ray.

"I guess I could if it won't be more than two hours."

"Great! Come on, kids!"

The screen door slammed.

From the window behind Ray's couch, Ann watched them go. What kind of woman leaves her sick father with a stranger? She sat down again and looked at her phone.

"Sorry," Ray said.

"It's all right. I don't mind keeping you company. Anyway, it's not your fault."

Two hours. Probably more with travel. She looked up the nearest movie theater. Thirty minutes away. That meant three hours.

"You'll be as bored as me."

"Want to look at this?" She picked up a picture book on the table. Palm trees on the front. And a thought occurred to her. Mercy Lake was close. Maybe fifteen minutes away.

"Ray, listen. I could take you somewhere. We can go to the beach. No palm trees, but it's not far. Just out. Just for a while."

Ray thought. "Impossible," he said.

"But if it wasn't. Would you want to?"

He smiled. "Sure."

She'd never get him out of the house. But he would let her have her fantasy. He couldn't allow himself to think about how wonderful that would be. He watched her, amused, as she stuffed things into a plastic bag: a towel, the pills from the end table, the bag of morphine. She took a moment to study him.

He had underestimated her. What she lacked in bulk she made up in determination. He helped her, as much as he could, to get himself first up with the walker, then slowly backed into the wheelchair, proud his legs would still hold his body in an upright position, if only for a few seconds before his own weight forced him into the seat.

"This isn't going to be easy." She glanced at the door. "Are you sure?"

"Yes," he said. He lifted his hand in a kind of wave that told her he was hanging in there.

"You can move, that's good," Ann said, and he was proud again. She was easy to please. He held onto the arms of the chair, trying to keep himself upright as she bumped him out the screen door.

He felt a small collision with a firefly. There were dozens of them in the dusk, floating alongside them as she wheeled him outside. He laughed when he realized they were a memory. There were no fireflies in October. Getting Ray into the car was precarious and meant crimping him into a sitting position and then pushing and pulling him onto the seat.

Now this was wakefulness.

She rolled the windows down. It had stopped raining by then, but the last week had seen torrents, and water was everywhere, pouring in streams from downspouts into metal pans, dripping from the eaves of houses onto beds of dry leaves. His hearing was acute. In fact, his ears seemed livelier than they'd been before the war.

The car stopped and moved and stopped. Streaks of neon came into focus above the darkened interiors of buildings he sensed more than saw. They were downtown. Then the motion became steady again, the sky dark and full of stars.

They stopped. Ann got out, cursed. She popped her head in the window.

"I need to open a gate here, Ray. I'll be right back, all right? All right?"

He lifted his head. She was illuminated by headlights, examining and yanking at a chain in front of her.

"Okay," she said and jumped back in the car.

They moved slowly for a short distance before coming to a stop.

"I've never broken into a park before," she said.

And the time passed, until three hours had come and gone.

A sound crept into his sleep and grew louder. Ray opened his eyes. It was morning now but bleak the way autumn can sometimes be. The dark had simply become lighter. There was no color in the world, except for Ann. She was vivid, hair brown, eyes blue, coat downy gray, skin pale like the dawn patches on the stand of birches at the edge of the beach. The sound came closer.

"Sirens. Jesus," she said. Her fingers tightened around his. "I'm staying with you, Ray."

"Go home," he whispered.

"What?"

There was a flicker of flashing lights in the rearview mirror, but for Ray, the sound had begun to recede, like sirens on a television in a neighbor's house.

He felt her fingers gently tucking the blanket around his chest. She got out of the car, and from the open window he heard her greeting.

"Officers," she said.

GUNSHOTS IN GRUDGEVILLE

I paced out twenty feet, which put me smack up against a birch tree, and raised the gun. After a long time trying to focus on the can instead of the sound of the wind in the trees and the shape of the clouds, I pulled the trigger. The first bullet skimmed the can. It made a little pinging sound but didn't knock it over. Still, not bad. I reloaded, feeling pretty sure of myself.

Thinking back, I'd swear I saw the brush move, and, even though it seemed to move in slow motion, there wasn't enough time to stop myself from pulling the trigger. I'll say this much: stoned or not, I had improved. The shot was dead-on.

In the newspaper clipping, my father smiles at the camera. His arm rests on the side of a brand-new motorboat, white with a bright red stripe along the body. He won it at the casino. As I pulled up to my parents' house, I expected to see it, but it wasn't there.

"Where's the boat?" I asked, pulling my hair into a messy ponytail.

"Unless you live smack-dab on a lake, a boat's just a pain in the ass," he said. "Once I showed it to everybody, I sold it. Got this instead." He lifted the garage door and looked at me. "It's used."

"No," I said.

"Not a thing wrong with it."

"It won't win any beauty contests," I said.

He shrugged.

The old pickup was the color of mustard and rusted around its edges. And almost as big as the boat had been. It barely fit in the garage. He squeezed himself along the wall and shoehorned into the driver's seat. Backing out took a full thirty seconds. The truck emerged from the garage like an old ship hauled up from the bottom of the ocean.

He tossed a rifle and a box of bullets onto the truck bed next to five- or six-gallon jugs of who knows what and a big garbage bag overflowing with empty Squirt cans.

"Well, what's the holdup?"

I hadn't even gotten my suitcase out of the car.

"Let me just lock up," I said, and pointed my key fob in the general direction of my little two-door. It beeped in response. Dad snickered.

I hoisted myself into the seat of the truck.

"Why not get a new truck?" I asked.

"Spend all that money? It's just for around here. Runs like new."

I noticed he said *runs*. It made sense. Something like that isn't really driven. It's operated, like a Panzer tank. He didn't talk about the war much, but the tanks had left an impression. He had nightmares about them was about as much as he'd say, and now he'd gone and bought the closest incarnation he could find.

The speedometer shivered at twenty miles per hour. No matter, he said. Anywhere he needed to go he could get to in a couple minutes, even at that speed. Half an hour at the outside.

We drove out of town the back way to get to our land in Grudgeville, which was not an official name, or even an official place really, more like a shack collection dropped onto the side of the road from God's big kettle, each with a ladle full of rusty machine parts right next to it, like its own side of beans. There's a legend about Grudgeville that says the people who moved up here from Kentucky didn't hold grudges, they buried them, right along with the people they had the grudges against. Crimes of passion, drunken brawls, cheating spouses, all buried in makeshift cemeteries or at the bottoms of little ponds you can't find unless you know the back roads as well as Dad does.

We drove by Lonnie Tritt's house, a mishmash of two trailers connected by a makeshift breezeway, and an old wheelbarrow planted with pansies and parked near the road next to the mailbox. He was tending to something in his yard. I strained to get a glimpse of him. Even from the road, his face looked out of proportion. You could tell something wasn't right. A year ago, he'd put a gun in his mouth, pulled the trigger, and still fell just short of killing himself. All because his daughter was pregnant, normally a happy occasion, but this grandbaby would be the offspring of a Mexican. A "dirty wetback," and the idea of Lonnie's pure breeding being messed with, well, it was the last straw in a long line of insults life had dealt him.

"Wow, Lonnie doesn't look so hot," I said.

"You should see him up close. Half his jaw's missing."

"Think it was worth it?"

"He don't have much up here," said Dad, tapping his forehead.

"'Specially now," I said.

Dad wheezed.

"I guess the truck didn't come with a suspension system," I said.

"Nope," he said, beaming. "Kind of like your brains are going to rattle right out of your eye sockets."

"Jesus," I said, and held on to the dash.

Three quarters of a mile in, the woods opened up to a clearing. On one side was a wooden shed built for equipment, with a roof extending out on one end to shelter the stacks of firewood built up over the summer. On the other, the land rolled down a slope covered in rows and rows of pine trees for selling at Christmas. I'd helped start the first batch. Hot, knee-busting activity with minimal gratification, at least for a kid. This latest he must have planted himself while I was living out of state ignoring my roots.

He took the padlock off the shed door and handed it to me.

"Hold this." He swung open the big door, letting out the smell of the straw that lined the floor of the shed.

"Gotta feed Penny."

"She's still around?"

"Yup, comes out whenever I call her."

Penny was a pheasant. She was brown. There wasn't much else to say about her, except that if a bird exits the forest when you cluck and eats corn right in front of you, it can also be called a pet.

"Hold this," he said and gave me a can with a little bit of corn and seed mix.

He closed the shed door. I hung the padlock in the loop to keep the door from swinging out on its own.

Even on this warm July day, Dad wore a pair of green workman's overalls from Fleet Farm. He owned half a dozen, because they were rugged. They came off once a year, exchanged for a sweater and pants on Christmas Eve.

We walked around to a small yard at the backside of the shed.

"Don't make any quick moves or she won't come out."

At the edge of the yard, a little worn spot held remnants of seed and corn from other days. Penny had gotten so used to the sound of seeds rattling around in the can he hardly had to call her at all. There was a slight waver in the brush, and out she stepped.

"Walks like your Aunt Gwendy," said Dad. "Always shows up for a meal, too." He started dropping seeds, a few at a time. Penny snapped them up as they fell.

When she was done, she turned back toward the woods and bobbed and strutted back into the undergrowth. He tossed a couple handfuls out for later, when she got hungry and he wasn't around.

We were there to shoot the twenty-two, something country people did to have fun, though I'd lived my life so far without doing it. Apparently, he thought it was high time. I followed him back to the truck for our weapons.

"Hold this," he said and handed me the gun and the Squirt cans.

"Did you bring the bullets?"

"Would I forget the bullets?"

"Never know," I said.

"Don't listen to your mother. I remember plenty," he said and lowered his voice. "When I want to."

"That's exactly what Mom said."

He ignored the comment and nodded at the gun. "Wait a minute now, don't shoot 'til I tell you."

"Is it loaded?"

"What do you think?" he said and walked around the backside of the shed again. He reappeared, rolling a huge stump with the top sawed off to a flat surface. Dad's nose was gleaming and red in the heat. He took a rag out of his overalls pocket and wiped his face.

"Whew, it's hot."

"Told you it would be," I said.

He grabbed a can out of the bag, walked over, and set it up on the stump. It looked small.

"That's a long way off," I protested.

"Then move closer."

I moved.

He snorted.

"Don't make fun of me," I said and waved the gun.

"Put it up on your shoulder, like so." He moved it a little from where I had it. "Now look through the sight."

"What?" I asked.

"At the end of the barrel."

"Where?" I asked again.

"Right there," he said.

I lowered the rifle and looked again.

He put his finger on two little metal prongs straddling the barrel. Between the prongs was a gap the width of a pinprick.

"I was expecting something visible. I can't see *that*, much less through it."

"Heck, I can see that," he said, "and I'm seventy-five."

I tried to look through it.

"You could always just aim it the old-fashioned way."

I started to laugh and had to reposition the thing again.

"Be careful."

I heard the pop of a can top behind me, smelled beer. I tried to stop giggling.

"Okay." I put the gun back on my shoulder and lowered my head. "I'm ready." I aimed.

"Now, pull the trigger."

I hesitated.

"You know where the trigger is, don't you?"

"Damn it, don't make me laugh." Once again I aimed. My first shot hit the stump.

He reloaded.

"Aim higher next time. Anybody can hit a stump, for Christ's sake."

I grunted, aimed, and missed again. Damn it.

He reloaded.

I walked closer, looking back at him out of the corner of my eye.

"Yeah, I see you," he said, shaking his head.

I aimed.

"Any closer you might want to just reach out and knock that can off there with your hand."

I was still about twenty feet away when I shot again and hit the can smack in the middle of the "u" in Squirt.

"Hah!" I said. "Look at that!"

"Let's see if you can do it again from more than a few inches back."

I adopted a stance.

All in all, I maimed twelve and killed three, the last from thirty paces.

"Well? How'd you do?" asked Mom while I washed my hands.

"Took her a while to figure out how to aim, but once she had that down, not too bad."

"Have you got any more bullets?" I asked.

"Sure. Out in the garage. Why, you want to go back out?"

"Maybe tomorrow. I can go by myself."

There was a pause.

"Dad. I'm thirty years old. I even changed a light bulb once."

"Do you know how to load it?"

Saturday was a beauty, as summer days go. Warm, breezy, big benign clouds floating by low enough to make shadows float over the village lawns. Onto the passenger seat went my backpack, my camera, a cold Squirt in the cup holder. And most importantly a couple joints in a baggie, still snug in the glove compartment. I threw the rifle and the cans in the trunk.

I parked in the clearing and got out. Quiet. Nobody around for half a mile. Something I missed now, that quiet. I inhaled, leaning against the car. The day stretched out in front of me with nothing specific to do, for the first time in a long time. I opened the trunk to get the gun.

Dad had moved the stump back to a little nook behind the shed. I rolled it a few feet out and set up my first can.

I should have told him right away. Wanted to. Meant to as I headed for home. But, when I turned the corner in front of Lonnie's place, I found the road blocked by a squad car. I reminded myself that our sheriff wouldn't drive clear across the county for a snip of marijuana even if he knew I had it. Ahead of the squad, I saw the unmistakable hulk of Dad's truck and a couple cars beyond that, all facing odd directions as if they'd screeched in at the same time in a hurry.

One of the three men standing in the road broke away and walked toward me.

"What's going on?" I whispered, because no one seemed to be talking except a voice near the house.

"Lonnie's got a gun."

"Again? Who would give that man a gun?"

The man laughed a little and adjusted his glasses, keeping his eyes on Lonnie.

I looked at him.

"You went to school with my son."

I pretended to recognize him. Funny how people could be part of your growing-up years, and then one day, their faces don't look at all familiar.

"Your dad's over there," he said.

Dad stood on the lawn in front of Lonnie's house next to a woman who was dangerously pregnant and not wearing much, just a white t-shirt stretched too taut over her belly and a pair of shorts straddling her hips. She must have been sweating; she kept wiping her hair from her forehead with the back of her hand. Everyone was looking up.

I gasped.

There was Lonnie, rocking precariously on the peak of the roof of his house, a leg dangling over each side, listening to his daughter explain that all babies are made by God no matter what color they are. Lonnie disagreed.

"Lonnie, this is booze talkin'," Dad said. "It doesn't make any difference what color that grandbaby is. What are you going to do? Shoot off something else? You're hardly healed from the first time."

Lonnie shook his head vigorously. "Marty, it ain't right."

"Come down now. Let's talk about it."

Lonnie steadied himself with his free hand. The hand with the gun swung down. The gun went off.

We ducked.

"Holy shit," I said, and Mr. Larson gave me a look I was free to ignore in my new incarnation as an adult, and I said it again just to drive the point home.

"It's just the truck. He hit that tire," yelled someone. We straightened slowly. I craned my neck to see the body of Dad's truck as it began a slow kneel to one side. *Uh-oh*, I thought.

"Get down! You're going to hurt somebody," Dad said.

"Okay, that's it," said the sheriff. "Marty, that's it. Move back."

Dad backed away slowly.

"You listen to me now. It's time to get down from there, you hear?" said the sheriff.

Lonnie lifted himself back into a sitting position and looked down. The hand with the gun waved in the air again.

"Drop that gun right now or I'm going to shoot. You understand me?"

All whispering stopped on the roadside.

"I've had enough. I don't want to shoot you in front of Linda, but I will if I got to. Just throw the gun behind you."

Lonnie dallied.

"Drop it! I'm giving you ten seconds."

The crowd gasped, and then all was still. I couldn't even hear a bird.

The sheriff raised his gun and aimed. "Ten . . . nine . . ."

Lonnie was too fast for him. In a sudden burst of consciousness, not to mention coordination, he lifted his arm. I must have turned my head then, because I don't remember seeing the end of the gun disappear into his mouth, or seeing Lonnie jerk back and fall. I only remember hearing the shot and the sandpaper sound his clothes made as his body slid down the shingles.

When I looked up again, the roof was empty. Mr. Larson was pale. He couldn't take his eyes off Lonnie, who was hung up in the shrubbery.

"Well, dammit," said Dad, and everyone watched as he walked back up to the road.

"You all right?" he asked me.

I nodded, though I didn't feel "all right," not at all.

"Go on home and tell Mom. Go on. I'll be there in a bit."

I got into my car. My muscles were like rubber bands. It took all my concentration to get my foot to stop wobbling on the gas pedal and push it down. I did a U-turn and went the other way, the long way, toward home.

Soon after, the sheriff and his deputy and Dad and I sat at the picnic table in our backyard. Dad put a few beers on the table.

The deputy shook his head.

"Did you see Linda? She got in her car and drove out behind the ambulance, not a tear coming down," he said.

"Why was he up there anyway?" I asked. "Why not out on the back forty or in his living room?"

The sheriff stopped mid-sip, like it was a dumb question.

"Where you been? Lonnie always shoots himself on the roof."

We laughed. It wasn't funny, but we had to try and make sense of a situation where there wasn't any to be made.

"Well, that's that, I guess," Dad said when they'd gone.

I couldn't bring up the dead bird *then*, for crying out loud. Dad was already upset.

That night I lay in my childhood bed, looking at the glow-in-the-dark stars on the ceiling that had been glowing my whole life, and cried. Not for Lonnie. It was the bird that had broken my heart. I thought about her out on the land, alone, wrapped in an old t-shirt. It could have been worse, I reasoned. She could have been injured and not dead. I'd had to leave her there; I couldn't put a dead pheasant in the back of my car.

"I'm sorry, Penny. I'm so sorry. I had no intention of killing you, goddammit," I'd said as I carried her into the woods, holding her close to keep the branches from snapping at her. On the crest of the hill under a tree, I laid her down gently and covered her with leaves and branches.

"Sorry, Penny."

I patted the little bump in the forest and made my way back to the car. I would wait to bury her until Dad had seen her.

I hoped Dad would eventually see the humor in the situation, or at least its entertainment value, and tell the story at the next family reunion with his eyes twinkling the way they do when he knows he's got a winner of a tale.

"And I musta' taught her too good," he'd finish, leaning toward his listener, "because she went and put a bullet in my pet pheasant the very next day!"

It might seem funny one day, but it sure as hell wasn't funny now. When I closed my eyes, I saw her, perched on the woodpile watching Dad split fresh cords, making little clucking noises at him he probably couldn't hear. Keeping him company. The more I thought about it, the more certain I became that he was going to be despondent over this for the rest of his life.

I slept uneasily. At dawn, Penny squawked at the edge of my consciousness and kept it up. I had to quiet that squawk. I pulled on my clothes and clunked down the stairs.

But Dad wasn't there.

He'd ridden his bike out to feed her at six in the morning, and she hadn't been there. She hadn't been there at ten, either. Pretty strange for a bird that had made regular meal calls for the last year and six months. He suspected foul play, because the Brown kids had been shooting around town for fun and taken out the Holcombs' dog the week before. I cursed under my breath.

There was something about that boundary, that turn off County T, that threw a switch, erased all the points I'd earned between now and then. I was back in my twelve-year-old mind, sneaking around the back of the church to hide a cigarette. I was ashamed to realize I was still hiding. A man was dead, and I was sweating over a bird.

A voice in my head said go tell him, for Christ's sake. Now.

But he was nowhere to be found.

I parked in the Browns' muddy yard, if that's what you'd call a mixture of mud and toys and car parts, and willed myself forward.

Molene and Kenny Brown sat on the screened-in porch like they had nothing to do in the middle of a Monday, which of course they didn't.

"Hey," I said, trying to smile, tapping on the screen door. I got no response, so I walked right in.

"Have you seen my dad?"

Molene sat, looking me over as if she'd never seen me before.

You are an asshole, I thought.

"Well, if it ain't little Bitsy Buzzykalewski, home from the big city."

Now if there is any kind of humor I hate, it's that kind. If I was Polish, why would I be insulted by my own name? If I was Polish, would the old battle-axe call me Rodriguez instead? I could think of a lot of things I wanted to say to that, like how it'd be better to be Polish than to be Molene, but Dad had to live here.

"He left here what"—she looked back at Kenny—"fifteen minutes ago?"

Kenny considered.

I got back in the car without saying goodbye.

"Don't let the door hitch ya on the way out!" shouted Molene.

I felt like giving her the finger.

Just when I'd almost forgotten what I hated about this place. To be fair, things had changed, just not much. It occurred to me that the big-city rudeness might be learned in small towns like this. After all, the cities are full of Midwesterners who arrived with their lack of manners. The locals might not believe it; then again most of them hadn't been anywhere else long enough to come back and compare.

Somewhere in town, my dad rode a bicycle, gunning for a bird killer, with no idea it was his own kid. *Dad the gumshoe.* I gave up. He'd show up at home.

I found Mom standing outside with her purse.

"Where's Dad?" I asked, trying not to shout at her.

"He's at the restaurant. Let's take your car."

Dad sat at a little booth in the back of the place with a big pot of coffee in front of him. We sat. I couldn't very well tell him about Penny in the restaurant. It was a miserable meal, with Dad peering over his menu at people he'd known most of his life. Fingering suspects.

Finally, he pushed aside a basket full of the bones of a quarter chicken and said, "Let's go home."

I drove slowly, following his bicycle over the railroad tracks, past the lumber mill, past the school. I pulled into the driveway behind him, dread filling my guts.

He waited for Mom to disappear inside and went to get a beer out of the garage. I fiddled with a couple of old tractor parts. The time had come.

"What's the matter with you? Looks like ya et a ghost," he said.

"Been a long few days," I said feebly, studying the posters of earth-moving equipment taped to the garage walls.

"Yeah, well, Lonnie had his mind made up. Put a couple beers on top of that, and there's not much can be done."

"Yeah."

"Guy couldn't face up to nothin' in life. Some people are like that, never grow up." He turned back toward his tool bench.

Jesus Christ.

"Dad, I killed Penny," I blurted.

He put his beer down and turned back around.

"It was an accident."

I explained, leaving out the pot. He didn't look mad. Confused, and not necessarily surprised. He half laughed.

"Well I'll be." He shook his head and took his cap off to scratch an ear.

"You're one quick study, daughter," he said, handing me a beer. "On shooting, anyway."

"She hasn't been interred yet," I said.

He thought about it for a while and took a swig of beer. His eyes glistened in the damp light of the garage.

"Let's go," he said.

I put both bikes away, and we got in the car.

The road was long in the early evening. Unsettled. Waiting.

It occurred to me we were headed toward Grudgeville to dispose of a dead body, just like a lot of people before me, if you believed the talk. Bird or no, Penny was part of the legend now.

ACKNOWLEDGMENTS

I couldn't have pulled this collection together without the support, hard work, and unwavering encouragement of Kim Suhr and Pam Parker.

I owe a debt to the Red Oak writing community and all the writers I've known—my creative family. So many teachers taught me invaluable lessons: Marge Pence, Dan Rosenberg, Nurit Tilles, Masood Akhtar. Dave Tronnier has been encouraging and reading my work for years, as have many other friends too numerous to list. I love you all and hope to support you in turn.

I'm also grateful for my best friend growing up, our town librarian, Audrey Gjelsten. Audrey instilled her love of books and stories into me, giving me the greatest gift, the desire to learn, explore, and to write.

And, last but never least, to my hometown, White Lake, WI, the inspiration for many of these stories.